THE SUMMER I
ROBBED A BANK

THE SUMMER I ROBBED A BANK

DAVID O'DOHERTY

Illustrated by CHRIS JUDGE

PUFFIN

PUFFIN BOOKS

UK | USA | Canada | Ireland | Australia
New Zealand | South Africa

Puffin Books is part of the Penguin Random House group of companies
whose addresses can be found at global.penguinrandomhouse.com.

www.penguin.co.uk
www.puffin.co.uk
www.ladybird.co.uk

Penguin
Random House
UK

First published 2021

003

Text copyright © David O'Doherty, 2021
Cover and illustrations copyright © Chris Judge, 2021

Danger is Everywhere extract: text copyright © David O'Doherty, 2014;
illustrations copyright © Chris Judge, 2014

The moral right of the author and illustrator has been asserted

Set in 11.75/20 pt Palatino LT Std
Typeset by Jouve (UK), Milton Keynes
Printed and bound in Great Britain by Clays Ltd, Elcograf S.p.A.

The authorized representative in the EEA is Penguin Random House Ireland,
Morrison Chambers, 32 Nassau Street, Dublin D02 YH68

A CIP catalogue record for this book is available from the British Library

ISBN: 978-0-241-36223-5

All correspondence to:
Puffin Books, Penguin Random House Children's
One Embassy Gardens, 8 Viaduct Gardens, London SW11 7BW

MIX
Paper from
responsible sources
FSC
www.fsc.org   FSC® C018179

Penguin Random House is committed to a
sustainable future for our business, our readers
and our planet. This book is made from Forest
Stewardship Council® certified paper.

For Swifty

1

I WILL NEVER ROB
ANOTHER BANK
EVER AGAIN

There's a feeling of relief that comes just after you've robbed a bank that's hard to compare with anything else. It's a bit like when you think you've forgotten your homework, and you'll be in HUGE trouble because it was a big project and the teacher is in a very grumpy mood today. But then, at the last second, you find it folded up in the part of your schoolbag where you never usually put anything. Well, it's a bit like that, but not really.

If you forget your homework, you don't get locked up in jail, or whatever happens when you're twelve years old and you've been caught masterminding a bank robbery. You are probably sent to a farm with barbed wire around it where they make you dig holes while snarling dogs look on.

As we turned off the road and rumbled up the driveway with the money onboard, I exhaled the longest breath I've ever exhaled. I felt the thick cloud of worry and tension that had been building up inside my body release into the world. I'm not sure I'll ever breathe a breath like that again because I don't plan on ever robbing another bank. In fact, I can absolutely and conclusively promise you RIGHT NOW that, for as long as I live, I won't even rob a pen from a bank.

So, before I forget any of the details, I want to write it all down. I want to try to make sense of what happened that summer and figure out how the quietest kid in his class at school, the worst worrier and the scarediest scaredy-cat became, for a while, one of the most wanted criminals in the country.

And, as with most things, the best place to start is right at the beginning.

2

REX (ME) AND UNCLE DERM

First I was born, and then they called me Rex, which I'm still not happy about. There are three main reasons I don't like being called Rex:

1. It's an eighty-year-old's name.
2. Or the name of somebody sitting on a horse in 1657 with a feather sticking out of his hat.
3. Or a dog.

It's the third one that bothers me most. There's a new thing every day.

'Hey, did you say your name's Rex?' somebody will ask. 'I'm afraid we have a no-chasing-cats rule in this library! Haha!' And then they always laugh for ages, like they're the first person ever to think of it and it's the funniest joke in the entire history of jokes.

'Your name's Rex? Please don't chew our shoes or pee on our carpet! Haha!' Usually with the *Haha* part going on much longer than that. More like *Hahahahaha*. And I feel my cheeks get hot and sometimes I panic and run away.

But I'm getting sidetracked already. My name is Rex, and that's not interesting, and we have a lot of *very* interesting stuff to get to. I'm called Rex because my granddad was called Rex. That's the entire fascinating story of why I'm called Rex.

YOU

ARE

WELCOME.

And, before you ask, NO, he wasn't a dog either. NONE OF US ARE DOGS! We're just regular humans, with eyebrows and thumbs and occasional fluff in our belly buttons.

I'm from Dublin, a city in Ireland, which, if you don't know it, is an island towards the top left of Europe that looks like a squashed-sideways teddy bear. The bear's legs stick out into the Atlantic Ocean, where the waves smash and wallop and the wind goes *hoooowwwl*. But Dublin is on the opposite side, where everything's a lot less dramatic. The waves ripple gently against the teddy's back and the wind barely ruffles his fuzzy fur.

None of what I'm about to tell you would have happened without two people:

- Kitty
  and
- Uncle Derm.

Let's start with my uncle. I'm told that I first met Uncle Derm when I was two, but I don't remember it so I'm not counting it. He lived in various exciting-sounding places around the world – Rio, Madagascar, Braintree. Then, when I was eight, he came back to Dublin.

Mum and Dad had always talked about Derm in an unusual way.

'That reminds me of my brother, Dermot,' Mum once said when we saw a rickety car with a door missing and a worn-out sofa tied on to the roof with string.

'That looks like somewhere Derm would live,' Dad would say when we passed a kind of homemade-looking house – one with bits stuck on to other bits and no overall plan. Maybe with an old satellite dish for a bird bath and a fence made out of radiators.

They must have tried every other possible babysitting option before calling him that evening. I didn't like babysitters, but especially not new ones.

'Anything could happen!' I said to Dad. 'Like what if he locks me in the attic or makes me fight a snake?'

'Rex, he's your uncle. You're being silly.'

So when I heard the doorbell, I did the thing I used to do when everything got too much. I lay, frozen stiff, on the stairs with my eyes clamped shut.

'I'm sorry about this, Dermot,' Mum said as she let him in. 'Rex is doing one of his shutdowns.' Then she leaned over me. 'Now, Rexypoos, be very good for Mummy and Daddy, won't you? If your tummy is hungry, there are some snackies in the fridgey.'

She went on, 'Dermot, can you make sure he's in bed by eight? This meeting ends at nine so we'll be back from the school by nine thirty.'

'Nine *twenty* if you let me drive,' Dad grumbled.

Mum snapped back, 'Your stupid brain probably doesn't remember, but the last time you drove you got us a flipping speeding ticket!'

Dad shot back, 'Maybe I couldn't concentrate because of you!'

'Maybe you were going the wrong way.'

'I'm surprised you could see what way we were going because you were yelling in my ear.'

As usual, their argument continued as the front door slammed shut behind them.

There was a moment of silence in the house, and then the first odd thing of the night happened: my new babysitter began to sing.

> *'There is my nephew Rex,*
> *Lying there*
> *On the stairs.*
> *Will he say hello?'*

I didn't make a sound.

> *'No.'*

It wasn't really a song, in that songs are supposed to be planned and written down somewhere. This was just him warbling away about whatever happened to be in front of him. I still hadn't reacted, but he kept going.

'I used to do this exact thing
When I was the same age as him.
But I think I can make him open his eyes
By giving him a big surprise.'

See what I mean? It was sort of funny, but mostly just annoying. Also, no way would I open my eyes now. NO WAY. Especially as he'd made the number-one mistake when trying to give somebody a surprise, which is to warn them that they are about to receive a surprise.

I heard Uncle Derm go outside to his van and then a sound like big plastic sheets being unfolded around me. All very strange, but I still didn't open my eyes. This was a shutdown, and shutdowns ended when I decided to end them.

Next, I heard long bits of tape being stuck to the walls and floor. Whatever this person was doing, Mum and Dad would NOT be happy. We lived in an INCREDIBLY tidy house. It looked like those fake rooms you see in the windows of big furniture shops.

I heard something being squeezed from a bottle and landing on the plastic sheets. What was it? Ketchup? *Yuck*. No, wrong smell, thank goodness. This was more lemony ... washing-up liquid, maybe? Then came the sound of the bath filling in the bathroom at the top of the stairs.

There isn't a word in this or any other book for the level of surprise I felt at what happened next, so I'm going to have to invent one:

shocksplosion
NOUN: the highest of all levels of surprise
The bigger the **s h o c k s p l o s i o n**,
the further apart the letters in it are.

First, I heard the unmistakable sound of what-ever the backwards version of a belly flop is called – a butt flop, I suppose – into the bath upstairs. *BLOOOB.*

A moment later, my eyes sprang open because a wave of warm bathwater had picked me up and slid me along the washing-up-liquidy plastic sheets, out through the open front door to under the hedge in our tiny front garden.

I considered going into another emergency shut-down right there, but for once I was too shocked for a shutdown. WHAT HAD JUST HAPPENED?

WHO

　　WAS

　　　　THIS

　　　　　　MONSTER?

My first sight of him came a few seconds later – his big face beaming out from under a mop of brown curly hair as he slid, feet first, through the front door on the temporary waterslide he had turned my home into.

'T-REX!' he bellowed as he came to a halt in the hedge beside me.

Ugh. T-Rex. That was the most annoying thing I'd EVER been called, and it was still only the fourth or fifth most annoying thing about this whole situation.

I tried to speak, but no sound came out, which is what happens when you've just been involved in a **s h o c k s p l o s i o n**. Thinking back now, it might even have been a

s h o c k s p l o s i o n.

'Great to see you!' Uncle Derm jumped to his feet, his clothes dripping. As he offered me his hand to shake, a stream of soapy bathwater flowed down his sleeve and directly into my open but still-speechless mouth. I coughed and, I don't know how, made a sound like a baby sheep: *'Mbaaagh!'*

Now he was trying not to laugh. He could see how angry I was, but the harder he tried to hold it in, the more his eyebrows twitched and his mouth started moving like he was sucking a very sour sweet. Soon his whole body was rocking like he was twirling an invisible hula hoop. He stumbled back a step, slipped and, as his wet bum hit the ground, it made a squelchy sound as if he'd landed on a pillow filled with jelly. And that made me smile, which made him giggle, and soon we were both rolling around in the wet, roaring with laughter.

'You can't do this!' I gasped, when I'd regained the ability to speak.

'Fair point,' he said, tears running down his cheeks. 'Maybe a bit late, though?'

'We're going to be in huge trouble,' I went on.

'Well then, let's tidy it all up right now!' He turned to go back inside.

'Wait!' I said, and my uncle froze in mid-stride. It seemed like a waste to have set all of this up and not to have another go. I mean, this was the same boring flight of stairs I shuffled up to bed every night and back down for school the next morning. 'Maybe I should try it one more time.'

'Now that's an excellent idea!' said Uncle Derm. 'And then I might have one more go too.'

We spent the first half of the rest of the evening taking turns to fill the bath and then slide down the stairs, and the second half trying to make it look like that's not what we'd been doing. We removed all of the plastic, then mopped, towelled and hairdryered the house and ourselves, right up until the moment Mum and Dad got back from the meeting. Then we both jumped on to the couch and switched on the TV.

'Sorry we're so late,' said Mum. Classic Mum – it was 9.32 p.m. '*Somebody* took a wrong turn.'

'*Somebody* gave me terrible directions,' Dad huffed as he stomped up the stairs.

'Rexypoos, you're supposed to be in your beddy-bye-byes,' Mum said when she saw me on the couch.

'Oh sorry,' said Derm. 'That's my fault. I wasn't paying attention to the time.'

'What have you been doing?' Mum asked as she hung her coat and briefcase on the coat stand in the hall, which a short time before had been a dangerously pointy outcrop in our fast-flowing rapids.

'Mostly nothing,' Derm said. 'Just watching this.'

He pointed at the nature programme on the television. A shark was chasing a seal.

'Dermot, I don't like him seeing stuff like this. It will give him nightmares! We really don't like anything to do with water, do we, Rexypoos?'

I didn't say anything, but Derm gave me a wink.

Just then Dad called out from the bathroom at the top of the stairs: 'Why are all the towels wet?'

The towels! The one thing we hadn't dried.

While I spluttered, trying to think of a possible reason, there came the ominous triple *rat-tat-tat* on the front door of Complainey Delaney, the world's complainiest next-door neighbour. Let's just say he never called in with wonderful news of wonderful things I had done.

I could only hear bits of what he was saying to Dad, and they were all bad.

'. . . water gushin' outta the house like a fountain . . . the two of 'em flappin' around like dolphins . . . and me, WORRIED I MIGHT BE DROWNDED.'

That evening was the one and only time Uncle Derm was asked to babysit. But it was also the evening he became my favourite person. Are you allowed to have favourite people? Your parents are your parents, and I didn't have any grandparents or brothers and sisters. But there was something about my uncle – he made extraordinary things happen. And things were about to get really extraordinary.

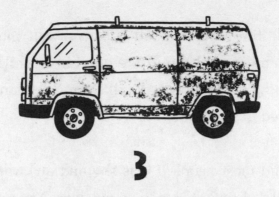

3

PARTNERS IN CRIME

I'd see Derm every few weeks. Sometimes he'd pick me up from school or we'd meet at a family thing – you know, New Years, new babies, new homes.

'Rexypoos, please make sure you and your partner in crime don't get into any trouble,' Mum once said as she caught Derm and me sneaking out of my perfect twin cousins' school graduation/every academic and sporting award/aren't-they-so-perfect celebration.

My partner in crime. I liked that.

One time, we climbed over the wall into the park and canoed round the pond in an inflatable paddling pool in the dark, till Derm fell in and got covered in swan poo.

Around most people I was shy and awkward. In school, I always ate lunch on my own. 'You need to come out of your shell, Rexypoos,' Mum would say, like I was a snail or an almond. But whenever I was invited to a party or a sleepover, she'd tell me I wasn't old enough. 'You'll just get scared and want to come home.'

I never felt shy or awkward with Uncle Derm. Sometimes we'd take his rattly old van on to the beach and he'd make me drive.

'Look at that dreary blob,' he said once, nodding over at the grey outline of Dublin City. Derm was at the back of the van, trying to push it out of some gloopy sand I'd driven us into. 'It needs people like us to give it some colour . . . GO!'

I put my foot on the accelerator and the wheels spun round so fast that they coated my uncle in a thick layer of sandy fudge. We laughed so hard we had to lean on things.

What was Uncle Derm's job? It seemed like he could do most things. He had trained as a carpenter, and then for a while ran a business that put huge inflatable things on top of other things – an enormous inflatable car on the roof of your garage, a giant croissant on your cafe. That was until a very large spaniel detached itself from the roof of a dog groomer's during a storm and landed on the railway track. On the news, the train driver said she'd thought it was a dinosaur and hit the brakes so hard that the train nearly came off the rails. That was the end of that particular spaniel and Derm's huge inflatable things business.

My uncle could make anything. Inside his van was every kind of tool and spare part. He'd go off to build a barge for somebody in Luxembourg, then he'd fix a windmill in France. He lost the tip of his left forefinger working at a zoo in Amsterdam.

'I'll tell you one thing I've learned, Rex,' he told me the next time I saw him. 'Never wrestle a panda. They look cute, but they can turn savage.'

'Really?' I said, shaking my head. I could always tell when he was making stuff up. It was the way he jutted his chin out just after he spoke.

'Well, it had climbed into the crocodile enclosure,' he went on. He knew I wasn't buying it and was trying to change his story.

'So hang on, was it a panda or a crocodile? Or maybe a panda riding a crocodile, like a horse and jockey?'

'OK, OK, you got me, Sherlock Holmes.' It turned out to have been an accident with a bench saw while he was building shelves in the zoo's gift shop.

Then Derm moved away again.

4

LOTS OF BAD NEWS
AND THEN SOME
GOOD NEWS

I want to get to the interesting part of this story, so
I'm going to fly through the next bit. Also, it's pretty
miserable.

I knew Derm hadn't been well. He didn't collect
me from school for a while, and then wasn't around
at Christmas. The next time I saw him was when he
called over for my twelfth birthday in February. He
looked a lot paler than before and his mop of brown
hair had all gone.

'I'm moving here,' he said, using the tip of a knife to point at an island just off the west coast of Ireland on the back of a ten-cent coin. 'Get some sea air in my lungs.'

When he saw how disappointed I looked by this news, he added, 'I'll be back every couple of months. You know what hospitals are like with their check-ups.' He took off his watch and put it on my wrist. 'Happy birthday, T-Rex.'

'But it's your watch!' I said.

He shrugged his shoulders and smiled. 'It'll remind you to come and visit.'

I asked Mum if I could go and see him during the summer holidays and she made excuses about not being able to drive me there, and how she had important summer jobs for me to do at home. 'And you'll be so excited about going to your new secondary school in September you won't want to do anything else,' she added.

She couldn't have been more wrong. I was going to a giant new school across town where I wouldn't know a single person and I was dreading it.

Then, in June, Mum and Dad split up. The worst part was they didn't even tell me. Well, they did, but only at the last minute. The school where Dad worked was closing down and he'd found a new job at a fancy school in America. He'd be moving there for a few years, till things picked up here and there were teaching jobs again. But he'd come back for the holidays.

I thought we were just dropping him at the airport. Then, in the place where you get coffee and those damp sandwiches in triangle boxes, he looked at Mum, and she looked at me, and she said it.

'Rexypoos, you'll have noticed that Dad and I haven't been getting on very well,' she began. Or I think that was how she began. I was reading the list of juices above the counter and renaming them with the worst possible names. *Pineapple Perfection?* More like *Pineapple Perploption*. Would anyone order it if it was called that? 'A Pineapple Perploption for me and a Blueberry Barf-Blaster for my friend.'

Anyway, she'd been talking, and I hadn't really been listening, until she said it: 'So we'll always be

Mum and Dad, but we aren't going to be together any more. How does that make you feel? Why are you smiling?'

I was smiling because I'd just invented a juice called a Blueberry Barf-Blaster, but also because I didn't know what else to do with my face.

I hate it when people ask you how you feel. I mean, I get it. They want to know if you're happy or sad or whatever. But when the thing has just happened, you don't know how you feel. They're just saying something to fill the silence. How do you feel when a car door opens in front of your bike and you fly over the handlebars? You don't feel anything. You just get ready for the big thump when you hit the ground.

I stayed in bed for the next few days. Mum brought me up food, and books from the library, but I wasn't hungry and I didn't want to read. It seemed like everything had changed and nothing would ever be the same again, and whether I ate toast or read a book about space didn't matter.

On the third day, Uncle Derm telephoned. Thinking back now, I bet Mum had called him and asked him to try to cheer me up.

He told me about his latest escapades on the island. The sheep that roamed everywhere had pushed over his fence and eaten the vegetables he was growing.

'So, to teach them a lesson, I dug up some of my carrots and soaked them in the hottest hot sauce it's possible to make. Rex, there was a skull and crossbones beside the recipe . . . Then I buried them back with the normal ones. Next time the sheep broke in: *Baa-AAAAGH, Baa-AAAAGH*. They ended up running all the way down to the sea, with their mouths open, and they haven't been back since.' His impersonation of hot-sauce baaing sheep made me smile for the first time in days.

He said I should come and visit, and I said maybe, but the truth was, even if Mum let me, I didn't feel like doing anything.

Then (and, thinking back, this is so awful it's almost funny) a week after Dad went away, Mum tripped over a gravestone at somebody I didn't know's funeral and broke her left leg in three places. She'd have to stay in hospital till the end of the month and Dad couldn't come back – he'd just started his new job in America.

So, when Mum gave me the option of staying with my perfect cousins or Complainey Delaney next door for two weeks, I said I'd go to Uncle Derm on Achill Island. Mum phoned Dad, and then phoned Derm, and that was that.

And this is where, you'll be glad to hear, everything finally gets going.

5

GETTING THERE

'T-REX!' roared Uncle Derm out of the window of his van, parked under a **NO PARKING** sign, across the rainy car park of Westport train station. I held my small blue backpack over my head and ran. The rain seemed wetter than the rain I was used to – the drops were blobbier. Like gravy rain.

I yanked open the passenger door and climbed in.

'It is SO good to see you,' he said, shuffling across the bench seat that spanned the width of his van to wrap his arms round me. For a moment, it felt like the roller coaster of the last month had stopped.

'Nice to see you too,' I said.

Derm looked thinner than he had on my birthday. His hair was starting to grow back, though now it was browny-grey. But his smile was as huge as ever.

'Oh my goodness, we are going to have the best time,' he said, sliding back across the seat. 'Mint?' He opened the green tin on his dashboard.

'Oh, no thanks,' I said. 'Mum says those ones are too strong for me.'

'Well, I don't see her here now,' said Derm, glancing round the van. 'I don't hear anybody calling you *Rexypoos.*'

'No, really,' I said.

Derm shrugged and popped two into his mouth, then turned the key. The van coughed a few times, but wouldn't start. He leaned over so his head was close to the centre of the steering wheel. 'Now, I have spoken to you about this in the past.' Most people are rude when they talk to things that aren't working. Not Derm – he was always so polite. He went on, 'Rex has just arrived and I want to get him to the island, so I'd really appreciate it if you could . . .'

The engine burst into life. Derm said thanks and soon we were rattling towards the exit.

'Do you need money?' I was already rummaging in my pocket for a coin to put in the slot beside the barrier to get out of the station car park.

'Oh no,' said Derm. 'These are free.' He dropped the two now-flat circular mints from his mouth into his hand to examine them. Then he sucked them back up, and for a few moments the only sound – apart from the engine – was the two mints clunking off each other in my uncle's mouth. From behind us, an impatient driver parped their horn.

Derm rolled down his window and waved apologetically. Then he narrowed one eye, selected one of the mints and placed it in the coin slot. He had sucked it down to the perfect size and the barrier rose in front of us.

'Let's go!' he said.

It was really gross, but – I have to admit – also very impressive.

As we left the car park, the wind blew the clouds away to reveal a new landscape. Huge, dark, dome-shaped mountains loomed around us. Where the fields had been flat green carpets on either side of the train, now they were bumpy yellow rugs, separated by walls of grey, mossy stones that looked like they'd been balanced on top of each other a very long time ago.

'I'm so sorry to hear about your mum and dad,' Derm said, and immediately I felt my body start to tense and my cheeks go red. I wasn't sure if I'd ever be ready to talk about it.

Derm must have sensed it was hard because he changed the subject. 'Tell me about my sister's leg.'

I could talk about that no problem. 'They put pins in it so she can't move for a month,' I said.

'Reminds you how lucky we are, Rex! We must be two of the luckiest people ever!'

He beeped his horn, which at first I thought was to emphasize his point, but blocking the road in front of us was an enormous cow.

My body froze. I'd never been this close to an animal that size. It was like a terrifying sofa with legs and a head.

'Has it escaped?' My voice trembled as I slid down in the seat.

Derm smiled. 'It must belong to a farmer near here. They stroll around.'

It stopped eating grass from the verge and turned to glare at us. I felt my heart beat faster and I began edging towards Derm.

'Is it going to flip us over?'

The idea made Derm laugh. 'They're very friendly but sometimes difficult to move. Give me that silver thing.'

He pointed at the array of strange items on the floor, under where I was now crouching – a flask, a snorkel and mask, a big mallet and a small, rectangular silver box, about the size of a thin chocolate bar. I passed it over and he leaned out his window and began blowing into it.

WAAAAWEEEEWHAWEEEEE!
WAHWHAHAHAHHWHA!

It was a harmonica – and Derm, it was immediately obvious, was NOT a harmonica player.

The cow was startled by this dreadful concert and began to move off the road.

'Sorry about that, madam!' Derm said, reaching out to pat her on the back as we drove by. 'It must be annoying when you're trying to have your lunch and someone drives through the middle of the restaurant.'

I'd looked Achill Island up in the encyclopaedia at home. There wasn't much.

'Achill is one of the three hundred and sixty-five islands of Clew Bay and the largest island off Ireland,' was the first sentence, which made it sound huge, till you remembered that Ireland is a not-very-big island itself. So it was the biggest small island off a not very big one. *'It's a mountainous place with a rich history.'* That was a little more interesting, although some eras of history (Vikings/dinosaurs) are clearly more exciting than others (Ice Age/the one where there was water everywhere and mostly just sponges).

Two and a half thousand people lived on Achill,

although that went up to four thousand during the summer. According to the map, it was twenty kilometres down and nineteen across at its widest point, and shaped sort of like a gun – a gun being held by the rest of Ireland, which, we've already established, is shaped like a squashed-sideways teddy bear. And, while it's dangerous for bears to have guns, there wasn't much for it to shoot. Just the vast liquidy expanse of the Atlantic Ocean.

A little further on, Derm pulled the van in at the side of the road and, for a moment, I thought we'd arrived. Then I remembered we hadn't seen the sea or an island yet.

'Not far to Achill now,' he said, nodding towards a sign at the fork in the road just up ahead that said **ACHILL ISLAND 30 KM**. He pronounced it 'A-Kill', not 'A-Chill' as I'd been saying it in my head.

Derm grabbed the mallet from under my feet. 'Just a second.' He jumped out and, with one mighty blow, made the sign point in the wrong direction.

'Why did you do that?' I asked as we drove on.

'Just a temporary diversion,' he said. And, before

I could ask any more questions, he burst into one of his terrible made-up songs:

> 'We're going to the most incredible place,
> It really will amaze your face.
> No, you won't believe your eyes,
> You'll say, "Eyes, seriously, what's going on, guys?"
> Each moment is like a diamond,
> When you're on Achill Islaaaaaaand.'

I shook my head. 'Eh, diamond doesn't really rhyme with island,' I said. 'And also how is each moment like a diamond? That doesn't make any sense.'

'I'm afraid you'll have to take it up with the writers of the song.'

'Oh yeah,' I said. 'Are they, by any chance, you?'

'Unfortunately, they are currently unavailable,' Derm responded.

'Just as long as they're not writing any more songs,' I said.

'Oh yes, they are. They will definitely be writing a LOT more songs.'

6

THE MONEY MACHINE

Now the houses were becoming more spread out, till there were just a few sprinkled on each hill or mountainside, and cows were outnumbered by sheep. Proper woolly, cloud-shaped sheep – the kind you'd draw if somebody handed you a pencil and said you had ten seconds to draw a sheep.

Derm whacked two more signs with his mallet as rain showers gave way to thick mist, then blue sky, then more rain.

'Does the weather always change like this?' I asked.

Derm nodded. 'Keeps you on your toes. Whatever's happening now, it could be the opposite in ten minutes. Always wear a waterproof coat, but have your swimming shorts on underneath.'

That was one garment I would NOT be wearing on this trip. Mum hated swimming and, to prevent me doing it, had taken the precaution of never buying me a pair of swimming shorts.

'Look, T-Rex – here comes the bridge!'

After an hour of driving, I was slightly disappointed. I'd imagined a creaky cable car or an old cargo plane. At the very least, a trip on a ferry, captained by someone who'd lost a body part to a shark. This was just a long, flat bridge, covered in cars.

'It's the only way on and off the island, and everyone's coming for the festival,' Derm said. 'It's also the longest swing bridge in the west of Ireland!'

'Wowee,' I said sarcastically, as if hearing bridge facts was my favourite thing. It was definitely the slowest swing bridge to drive across in the west of

Ireland, as the line of cars in front of us was moving at a sheep's walking pace.

As soon as we were back on solid ground, he roared, 'Welcome to Achill Island!'

I sensed another song might be coming so I interrupted. 'I need a bank machine.'

'What?' Derm seemed startled.

'You know, a money machine.' I mimed putting a card in and pressing buttons. 'A machine that you get money out of.' Now I was just saying the same thing, but using slightly different words. 'In case there's an emergency and I need to buy anything.'

'I understand what money is,' said Derm, 'but unfortunately there isn't one of those machines on the island. I can give you money if you need it.'

'What's that?' Up ahead, parked at the side of the road, was a vehicle about twice the size of Derm's van with **IRISH NATIONAL BANK MOBILE SERVICE** written on the side.

Derm stayed silent as we came towards it.

'It says it's a mobile bank,' I said. 'Is it, you know, a mobile bank?'

'Oh yeah,' Derm muttered. 'There is that. But it's not open, I'm afraid. It drives round the island Fridays and Mondays, so we'll catch it another time.'

As we passed by, a woman was stepping out of the door at the back, counting money. Behind her a sign said **OPEN**. I looked at Derm.

'Maybe it is actually,' he said. 'I'll pull in here so you can check.'

But Derm didn't pull in there. He kept going a couple of hundred metres up the road and parked behind a hedge.

'I'll wait here,' he said, 'out of the wind.'

I trudged back in what at first was wind, which then became windy rain. When I reached the mobile bank, I took a deep breath. I got nervous in new situations and I'd never seen anything like this before. It was halfway between a camper van and a delivery truck, with the door of a regular bank at the back. I counted from three, took another deep breath and pulled it open.

Suddenly I was standing in the calm of a perfect, tiny bank. While the wind gusted outside, a clock tick-tocked on the wall beside a wooden rack of leaflets advertising different accounts and a display of Niall the Gnome's Kidz Klub moneyboxes. In front of me were two customers and a pointy-faced bank teller with a thin moustache who was impatiently pulling money from a drawer underneath the counter.

'Twenty, forty, sixty – ah, count it yourself. I'm pretty sure it's all there.' He shoved the pile of money across the counter.

Behind him, facing in the opposite direction, I could see the bearded van driver, dressed all in dark blue with a peaked cap. He was reading the newspaper he had spread out across the steering wheel.

The next customer was a lady who placed two heavy green bags, overflowing with notes and coins, on the counter. Pointy gave a loud tut. 'This festival is the worst.' You can always tell when someone hates their job, and Pointy seemed to hate every part of his.

The lady, though, seemed happy. 'Hopefully, it'll be even busier this weekend!'

'Hopefully not,' Pointy snapped back. 'You've counted them?'

She nodded as she filled in a form and he stamped a big red ink stamp on it, before tossing the bags into a cupboard beneath the drawer. 'Next!' he yelled, and I approached nervously with my bank card in my hand.

'Hello, can I . . .' I was hoping he wouldn't start a conversation, but when I saw him reading my name off the card, a smile crept across his face, and I knew what was coming next.

'This one's called Rex!' Pointy bellowed at the driver. Then he turned back to me and lowered his voice. 'Just so you know, you can't do any barking in here or rub your bum on our carpet.' Then a little pause before the worst part – 'Hahahahaha!'

Driver turned round to join in.

'Rex, if you could not chew any of the leaflets or the moneyboxes . . .' Pause. 'Hahahahahahahahaha!'

I felt my face burn bright red. Now I just wanted to get out of there, but I needed money . . . What if something awful happened and I couldn't buy food or a stick to defend myself from a cow attack!

'Can I get twenty, please?' I mumbled, while staring down at the counter.

'What?' Pointy said. 'Speak up, Rex.'

'Normally, dogs are too loud,' said Driver.

'Twenty euro, please,' I said.

'Now I hear you!' Pointy took my card and stuck it halfway into the machine with the keypad. 'Pop your number in there.'

I felt a draught of wind and glanced round to see another customer enter with more bags of money.

My number ... what was it? Now my brain was refusing to cooperate – 0-0-0-0 was the original number when they'd sent me the card. But what had I changed it to?

It had been 1-8-0-2, the eighteenth of February – my birthday – until I saw something on the news about how birthdays are too easy to guess ... Was it 1-2-3-4? No, too obvious – 4-3-2-1? Not obvious enough.

Panic was rising inside me. I looked up at Pointy's face, hoping it would trigger something.

'I have an idea,' he said with a smirk. 'Maybe it's *woof-woof-woof-woof*?' Then he laughed again. 'Hahahahaha!'

'I have an idea,' said Driver. 'Maybe it's *HOOOOWL*.'

Suddenly my head was filled with random combinations of numbers.

9-1-3-5? 8-2-3-0?

I felt everybody's eyes glaring at me, and when the woman behind me coughed it was suddenly too much. I reached over, pulled my card from the machine and ran out of the door back into the blustery . . . oh. Now it was sunshine.

Derm could tell I was flustered when I got back to his van, but he didn't make a big deal about it. He didn't tell me to calm down or that I needed to come out of my shell. He just handed me a twenty-euro note. 'Ask me if you need any more.'

And that was it. That was why I loved my uncle.

7

A VERY BAD
FIRST IMPRESSION

We drove towards a banner draped across the road:

**ACHILL ISLAND SUMMER FESTIVAL
16TH TO 23RD AUGUST**

'This is the biggest week of the year for tourists,' said Derm. 'They'll all be fishing, surfing, hiking, biking. It'll quieten down after the weekend.'

It still seemed pretty quiet. Sitting on a bench outside the pub we were passing, a man was asleep on top of his dog.

'We're just a bit further,' said Derm.

I'd grown suspicious of the word *just* on this journey. He'd said that Achill was *just* past the train station, and then his cottage was *just* over the bridge. But, as the van came over the next hill, Derm said, 'You have to guess which house is mine.'

'Not that one,' I said. The first was a neat, boxy cottage with a perfectly square cut hedge around it. It looked like somewhere Mum and Dad would live . . . or somewhere they would have lived.

'This one's too big,' I said as we approached a long building with a line of about twenty windows and a short tower at one end. Paint was peeling off its walls and you could see grass growing out of the roof. 'What is it?'

'This is the most important building on the whole island. It's the Old Coastguard Station. I've been up on that roof, trying to fix holes, for the last week,' said Derm, slowing the van right down.

'Do old coastguards live there?'

'Coastguards used to live there. Now it's the assisted-living centre for the island.'

'Is that like a hospital?' I asked.

'No, but there's a doctor and quite a few nurses. Some of the people there are old and don't have long to live; others just need some help. Kathleen's recovering from a hip operation. Prem had an accident a few months ago and lost his sight.'

It looked like the building needed some help too. 'Why don't they just go to the hospital?'

Derm gave me a look. 'Because the hospital is far from the island – and people should be able to stay in the place they love . . . Uh-oh!'

He jumped on the brake again. This time it wasn't a cow. A large red-faced man with a flap of bright red hair bouncing off the top of his head had run out in front of us, and he was shaking his fist at my uncle.

'Beautiful day, Mr Angley!' said Derm, rolling down the window.

'You!' the man rasped, and then sucked in another

lungful of air to convert into fury. 'The building inspector has just telephoned FROM GALWAY CITY.'

'A lovely spot,' said Derm calmly.

'It's one hundred miles over there!' Mr Angley screamed and gestured wildly in the direction of Very Far Away. Then he jabbed a finger at Derm. 'He got lost because SOMEBODY pointed all the road signs in the wrong direction.'

'Probably the wind,' said Derm, smiling.

'Probably the same person who telephoned him and told him not to come last week, and who, the week before, when he did come, put a sign that said "Old Coastguard Station" outside the library.' His face had now gone from red to beetroot.

'Mr Angley.' Derm was speaking very slowly and that seemed to annoy Angley even more.

'WHAT?'

'I am welcoming my nephew to our beautiful island, and you're giving him a very bad first impression.'

Mr Angley ignored this and leaned into Derm's face so that their noses were nearly touching. 'I am going to personally collect the inspector tomorrow, and there's nothing you can do about that.' He kicked Derm's wheel and immediately grimaced. It had hurt him more than it had hurt the van.

'Have a majestic journey,' said Derm with a sweep of his hand, and we drove on.

'What was all that about?' I asked.

'Oh, just an old . . . well, not really a friend. He's a neighbour and we're having some disagreements over a refurbishment – well, more of a demolition . . .'

'Of the Old Coastguard Station? I thought you said it's the most important building on the island?'

'These things will all work themselves out in the end, I'm sure,' said Derm. 'Now, as I was saying, which house is mine?'

The next one had a fancy old sports car parked in the garden and a well-behaved labradoodle sitting by the front door.

'No way,' I said.

Then something caught my eye – a burst of colour beside the road. It was a fence with panels painted red, orange, blue and green, which, as we got closer, I realized was a bunch of old radiators that had been attached together.

'THIS is your house!' I shouted.

'You know me so well!' said Derm with a chuckle. He turned off the road and pushed the gate open with the front bumper of his van.

We rumbled up a steep, stony driveway for about thirty seconds and we were there.

I jumped out and looked around. From up here on the hill, there was so much colour: the blue ocean, the green mountains and the yellow valleys popping with purple and orange wild flowers.

'I searched the world for the place I wanted to spend the rest of my life, and I found it here. What do you think?'

He was happy when I nodded. 'I like it,' I said.

I'd never seen a picture of his house, but this is exactly what I'd expected. What had once been a small cottage had bits added in all directions. And, to the side, he'd built a giant wooden shed, big enough to park his van inside.

'Uh-oh. Have you been robbed?' I asked, pointing at the wide-open front door of the house.

Derm laughed. 'You're not in the city now, Rex. It's always open. Follow me.'

Through the front door was a tall sitting room, and hanging from the walls and ceiling were hundreds of brightly coloured objects: big ball-shaped floats in pink and yellow, huge blue seashells and green glass bottles.

'All washed up on the beaches,' Derm said. 'Like you, I suppose. I found you washed up under the hedge in your front garden.' This made me smile.

'You're in here.' He pointed to a door underneath a big plastic ice-cream cone with Spanish writing on it.

I tried to open it, but the door wouldn't budge. Then it moved a little but was banging against something – or was something banging against it? Derm tried, and we both definitely heard movement inside – tiny footsteps, even some breathing. Then a noise that at first sounded like a baby, but then definitely not a baby.

'I bet I know who this is,' said Derm, shaking his head, before forcing the door open with his shoulder.

Squashed together inside my bedroom were twelve sheep, and bouncing on the bed was a girl, a little older than me and much taller. She had on a white T-shirt and yellow trousers with one knee missing and, each time she bounced, her brown wonky plait would land on the opposite shoulder. On her feet were white tennis shoes that were so worn they were almost sandals. She was beaming broadly. 'Hi, Rex! I'm your neighbour, Kitty. Welcome to Achill Island!'

I took one look at her, then down at the sheep, turned and ran back outside. I climbed into Derm's van and locked the door.

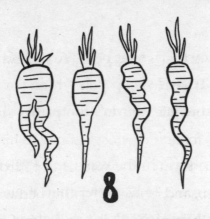

8

ALL TOO MUCH

'Come on, T-Rex. She was just trying to be friendl–
aahCHOO!' A cloud of smoke had gone up Derm's
nose as he leaned over the barbecue he'd made from
an old satellite dish.

I was sitting on the ground behind the shed,
looking down at nothing. After my unexpected
welcoming ceremony, I had curled up on the front
seat of Derm's van for a few hours till the sheep –
and the sheep girl – were definitely gone.

'Oh, come on, please talk to me,' he said. 'This is
like when you were a kid. You used to do that thing
where you went silent.'

'A shutdown!' I snapped. 'And this is not a shutdown. There's sheep poo where I'm supposed to sleep and some weirdo's footprints all over my bed.'

'Your sheets are in the wash and I've cleaned up the rest. It's going to be better than it was because, to be honest, it wasn't that tidy before. Here, take this.' He held out a plate.

While I was still annoyed about what had happened, I was also very hungry, so I stood up and took the plate.

My uncle scooped some objects from a steaming pot he'd brought out. I say objects because none of them looked how vegetables are supposed to look. I know you're not reading this book to hear my detailed descriptions of root vegetables, but let me just tell you about the carrots. Carrots, I'd been brought up to believe, were pointy orange rockets of vegetable goodness. These were like witches' noses. And they were yellow.

'Grown three metres from where we're standing,' Derm said proudly, pointing up towards his vegetable patch with the mini-digger parked beside it. What gardener uses a digger? 'They're not like the ones from the supermarket,' he added.

He was right about that.

Then it got worse. He reached over with his tongs and plonked a fish down on my plate. I need to be very clear here: I don't mean the tasty part in the middle, maybe with the risk of a few bones here and there. Or the crispy golden fishy pencil case you get with your chips at the local chipper. I mean a WHOLE fish: fins, gills, tail, mouth, bum and that big eye staring up – an eye that seemed to be saying, *'When I woke up this morning, I did NOT expect this.'*

It was all too much. I thought of Mondays at home, which used to be pizza and a board game with Mum and Dad, and my eyes began to fill with tears.

Derm put his arm round my shoulders. 'Come on,' he said. 'I'm taking you on an adventure.'

9

A SENSE OF WHOA

'It's my *Titanic*,' said Derm.

Fifteen minutes after the fish incident, he was sitting in his boat, untying a rope from the crumbling pier it was attached to.

'Well, it's lucky that nothing bad ever happened to a boat with that name,' I said, tightening the straps of the much-too-big life jacket he'd given me. I was standing on the pier, still deciding if I'd join him onboard.

'This is the quiet side of the island,' he explained. 'Not the one that faces the Atlantic.'

'Is it safe?' I asked.

'Sure it is,' Derm said, adding, 'compared to a lot of other stuff.'

Two things here:

1. There was only one sort of safe I was interested in and that was VERY.
2. 'Compared to a lot of other stuff'? What stuff? Maybe lion dentistry or bomb juggling?

The only boat I'd been on before was the very large ferry to Wales, and then my mother's anxiety about us being at sea had been reduced by the selection of films at the onboard multiscreen cinema.

'Sometimes it's good to open yourself up to new things, you know?' Derm said. 'Get out of your comfort zone. Find the things in the world that fill you with a sense of –' he searched for the right word – 'a sense of whoa.'

'But what if I'm happy with the things I like already, and I don't want to like any more things?' I said.

'How will you know if you don't try?'

Five minutes later, I was onboard.

'It's called a currach,' Derm explained as he pulled the cord to start the engine. 'It's the traditional boat of these parts They've been the same for a thousand years – well, except for the engine.'

It was about a metre wide and four metres long, with no cabin or place to shelter. Definitely no cinema.

Derm could see that I was nervous. 'It's flat calm,' he said.

While there was no wind, I wouldn't have described it as calm. If this had been a lawn, you couldn't have played tennis on it.

'Where are we going?' I asked.

Derm shook his head. 'You see, that's how I used to think: *Where are we going? When will we be back?* That's what living in the city does to your brain, T-Rex.' He tapped his finger on his head for emphasis. 'Let's just get out on the water and see where it takes us!'

As we chugged away from the pier, I noticed a tall, rectangular building beside it.

'Is that a factory?'

'A factory!' muttered Derm, shaking his head. 'It's the pirate castle.'

'A pirate castle! How old is it?'

'Old-old. Fifteen something . . .'

I clearly wasn't dealing with an expert here. 'Who lived there?'

'The Pirate Queen of Achill.'

'Yeah, right.' Once he'd told me that burps were caused by eating haunted food and I said it in class the next day, and for the rest of that year they called me Ghost Burps. But, still, I couldn't help asking, 'What sort of Pirate Queen?'

'What do you mean, what sort of Pirate Queen? She was a pirate, who was also a queen of the island and the area around it. That sort of Pirate Queen.'

I had so many more questions, but I knew we'd reached the limit of my uncle's knowledge on the subject. I knew that because he started singing:

> *Two guys out at sea,*
> *In a wooden boat.*

Let's hope it doesn't sink
Because guys don't float.

They'll keep on going
Until it starts to get dark,
And hopefully
They'll see a shark.'

'Excuse me?' I must have misheard the last bit.

'It's the right time of year,' said Derm, while making his eyebrows go up and down. 'There are loads of them around at the moment and they swim near the surface so you can usually see . . . LOOK!' He was pointing off behind.

I inhaled a deep breath. I didn't want to look round, but I couldn't help myself, in the same way you can't not watch a football heading towards a window. It wasn't a shark, thank goodness. Roaring towards us was a much bigger blue-and-orange boat, with a cabin at the front and a spotlight mounted on the roof. On the side was written **Achill Island Lifeboat**, and three men and two women in blue overalls stood on deck.

'Are they coming to rescue us?' I asked.

'Rex, we don't need to be rescued. We are having a nice time. They're just doing a patrol.'

As they passed, a crew member gave Derm a little wave, and Derm dramatically saluted back in a way that let you know he'd never been in the navy.

As we watched the lifeboat continue up the coast, my eye was drawn to a dark lump in the water up ahead. 'Lucky they didn't hit that rock,' I said, before the awful realization sank in that it was moving slowly in our direction.

'You've spotted one!' said Derm excitedly.

I felt my cheeks go red.

But, instead of steering us away from it, Derm shut the engine off.

'WHY DID YOU DO THAT?' I yelled. 'We need to get out of here!' Suddenly my palms were drenched in sweat.

'Shush,' said Derm. 'We don't want to scare it.'

Us scare it? When he saw the panic on my face, my uncle tried to calm me. 'It's a basking shark, T-Rex. They're the second-biggest sharks in the world but they're so gentle!' And, when he saw that I looked even more worried now, he added, 'Even if you fell in on top of it, it couldn't eat you. Its teeth are too small.'

None of this was helping.

The thing about most s h o c k s p l o s i o n s is that they're over in a second. It goes:

ORDINARY LIFE – s h o c k s p l o s i o n –
BACK TO ORDINARY LIFE.

But this one started as a shock, and then the shock got bigger and bigger. I think it might have been a *s h o c k s p l o s i o n*.

I was now so far away from my comfort zone that I wasn't sure I'd ever find my way back. Especially when my uncle whispered, 'Hello, Sharkey!' over the side of the boat.

I peered over and saw it swim past. It was a long, dark grey shape, maybe twice the length of our boat, with puffed-out gills and a triangular fin midway along its back, propelled by a gently swooshing tail.

Suddenly I was panting like I'd run a race. I looked up at my uncle, with eyes the size of moons. 'That's . . . incredible,' I said. I hadn't chosen the word. It had just come out.

He nodded enthusiastically. 'It's good to be reminded of how tiny we are.'

But it wasn't over. As soon as it had passed, a second shark, about one third the size of the first, glided by.

'Look!' I said.

'Must be a mum and her kid,' said Derm.

'Where's the dad?' I asked.

'Maybe he's gone to work in America,' said Derm with a smile. Then he started the engine and we set off again.

'Are you having a nice time?' Derm asked a few minutes later. 'I can't really tell from your face.'

I thought for a moment. While I'd been terrified not long ago, now I was starting to relax and look around. 'I think I might be,' I said.

Up ahead, the stretch of water we were travelling along began to narrow.

'That's the bridge we crossed earlier,' said Derm. It looked enormous from this angle, with huge steel posts going down into the water to hold it in position. Soon we were directly under it and Derm shut off the engine again. 'Listen,' he said.

When a car travelled over us, it made the whole bridge vibrate.

'What are we doing?' I asked.

'I have one quick job to do. Keep an eye out and tell me if you see anybody watching.'

Derm waited till there was complete silence, then removed a pair of pliers from his back pocket and stood up. 'Just give me one moment . . .'

He opened a steel electricity box that was mounted on one of the posts and began fiddling with wires. One sparked as he touched it and gave him a small electric shock.

'Are you definitely supposed to be doing this?' I asked anxiously.

'Oh yeah,' said Derm. 'You see, once in a while the bridge needs to be opened.'

'And you're definitely the right person to do it?'

'Well, I don't see anyone else around here,' Derm responded with a smile.

Suddenly a motor inside the bridge whirred into action and the whole section above us began to move. It was swinging to the side like an enormous gate.

'A swing bridge!' said Derm for the second time that day, and now I understood.

He took a tube of glue from his pocket and squeezed it round the edge of the box, then carefully pressed the door shut again.

'Why are you doing that?' I asked.

'Just sealing it up so nothing can get in. At least for a day.' He turned the boat round and motored us back towards the pier, at twice the speed we had come.

*

I was so hungry when we got back to the house that I ate a handful of Derm's strange vegetables right out of the pot. This time it was dark, so I couldn't see them. He was right: they did taste better than the ones from the shop.

'Let me see that fish,' said Derm. He took my plate from earlier and, with a few expert cuts, removed the head and the bones. I ended up eating everything that was left. Even though it was cold, it tasted delicious.

As I lay in my new bed, I felt exhausted, but also exhilarated – pirates, sharks, boats, all in an evening. Normally, I couldn't sleep in beds that weren't my bed, but this felt snug.

But as I dozed off, one thought kept coming into my mind. If we had no plan when we set off in his boat, why had Derm brought his pliers? Had he always intended to open the bridge?

I'd find out very soon.

10

PURPLE HAZE

My favourite time of day isn't when I'm awake or asleep, but the short in-between bit. The few minutes just before dozing off or just after waking up when I'm not sure what's real and what's a dream. Ideas bounce around my head like the balls in the lottery.

So, when I opened my eyes on my first morning in Derm's house, I wasn't too surprised to find that my room had disappeared. There was just purple – a solid fog of it all around. *Maybe I'm a seagull in a cloud, or an Achill pirate up in the crow's nest on a foggy evening,* I thought. This was definitely a dream.

But, looking down, now I could see my duvet. It had a thin grey stripe pattern, and one of my feet was sticking out the end. This was odd because, in dreams, you don't usually have boring details like sticking-out feet, or the clock beside your bed. After another moment, I could see my blue backpack on the chair. Maybe a lion was about to leap out of it or its zip would become a mouth and start talking . . . *AHCHOO, AHCHOO!* I sneezed twice. Wait, the purple fog was making me sneeze. Maybe this wasn't a dream.

I got up to investigate. It was purple in the sitting room too, and right out to the front door. Outside, I couldn't see the sea or the mountains in the distance. Just purple.

'HELLO!' A terrifying head appeared in front of me. 'Did we wake you?' It was human in shape, but had a pane of glass where its face should be.

Wait, this must be a nightmare!

'Oops!' Something bumped into me from behind. I whirled round and Derm was standing in his dressing gown, carrying a tray with a teapot and two mugs. He gave a big yawn. 'Morning, T-Rex. Sorry I'm not dressed. I had to go out and do one more thing after we got back last night and I'm absolutely exhausted.'

This wasn't a nightmare: it was just a *very strange morning*.

'Let me introduce you to Ronan. Ronan, this is my nephew, Rex.'

The purple smoke was drifting away to reveal an extremely tall man with arms and legs that looked like they belonged to an even taller man. He'd been holding a drawer in his hand, but dropped it on the ground as he struggled to remove what I could now identify as a snorkel and mask from his face. I remembered it from the floor of Derm's van. As he pulled the mask off, the elastic strap bungeed down past his camouflage trousers and wound itself round one of his shoes. As he tried to shake it off, he tripped over the drawer and stumbled towards me. I had to grab him around the waist to stop him falling over.

'I'm Ronan. Very nice to meet you, Ray,' he said as we kind of hugged.

'His name's Rex,' said Derm.

'And you've come here all the way from Dundalk,' Ronan went on.

'Dublin,' Derm said.

'And your mother fell into a grave at a funeral.'

'Close enough,' said Derm, with a shrug.

'You should call in for my daughter Kitty. We live right next door.'

In Dublin, right next door meant on the other side of your wall. Here, the house he was pointing at would have taken at least five minutes to get to. I nodded and said maybe, even though I would rather have eaten a wasp than make friends with that sheep girl.

Nobody seemed unduly worried about the purple smoke that was pouring out of Derm's shed. 'Is that . . . on fire?' I asked.

'Oh no,' said Ronan. 'That's just –'

Derm cut across him. 'We've been testing these new distress signals. You know, for boats that get stuck at sea. So helicopters can see them and whatnot.'

'But why were you wearing a snorkel?' I asked.

'Very good question, Ray,' said Ronan, and he looked over at Derm.

'We wanted to see what conditions would be like if one went off while you were wearing a snorkel,' Derm explained. 'How was it, Ronan?'

'Purple.'

'How purple?' probed Derm.

'Very purple.'

Derm nodded. 'As I suspected.' And before I could ask any more questions he said, 'So that concludes today's testing. Let's have some tea and biscuits and discuss our results.'

As they went inside, I looked up at the purple tower of smoke in the sky. Something very strange was happening that nobody wanted to tell me about.

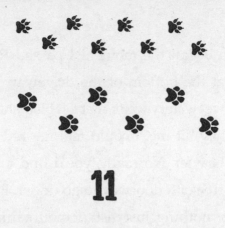

11

A DOG AND A CAT

'Where's the telephone?' I asked my uncle when I'd got dressed. The smoke had cleared and he and Ronan were at the kitchen table, hunched over a map and deep in a hushed conversation that stopped every time I came into the room. I went on, 'I should ring Mum and let her know that I've, you know, got here.'

'Oh sorry, T-Rex. I don't have one and mobiles don't work on the island,' Derm said, looking up. 'But there's a payphone at the shop beside the bus stop.' He motioned in a general leftward direction, before looking back down at the map again.

*

The rain began the moment I passed Ronan's car, parked at the bottom of the driveway. Big blobby blobs of wet watery water that left blob-shaped marks where they hit me. I could feel my red sweatshirt getting heavier. Normally, you'd find a bus shelter or a big tree or a doorway to go under. But out here there was nothing. Just distant mountains and fields of cows and sheep. I spotted a bush growing over a fence across the road, but, as I inserted myself under it, a terrifying screech came from just behind my left ear.

'EEEEEEEEEE!'

I whirled round and found myself staring into the dark eyes of a horrific beast-monster. It could be a bull! OR EVEN A RHINO! At any moment it could smash through the fence and . . . I sprinted off down the hill, splashing through puddles as the rain bucketed down.

I ran until I couldn't run any more, and slumped against a metal pole at the bottom of the hill. As I checked behind to make sure that the beast wasn't still charging after me (it wasn't), I noticed that I was leaning against the stop for the bus to Westport train station. I had reached the shop.

From the outside, it didn't look like any shop I'd seen before. It was like one from a museum display entitled *What things used to be like*. There were rusting signs for drinks that didn't exist any more: **Drink ZESTY orangeade**, **TRY TUESDAY TROPICAL PUNCH**. Stickers on the door advertised newspapers that had gone out of print years ago.

In the window, a display tipped you off to the chaos that awaited inside. A box of breakfast cereal advertising a film I didn't remember had a half-melted Easter egg balanced on top of it as a head (this was four months after Easter) and two rolls of kitchen paper under it, as legs. Its toothpaste-tube arms had fallen off a long time ago and lay by its sides.

I couldn't see the payphone outside, so I took a deep breath and pushed the door open.

It was a few seconds before my eyes adjusted to the darkness, and a few more to make sense of what I was seeing. There was absolutely no plan to this shop. Cans of tinned soup were mixed up with tins of paint and tennis balls. Bottles of shampoo sat on shelves beside dog food and nappies. I took a few more steps forward. There was no sign of the shopkeeper, but an awful screeching violin sound was coming from upstairs.

While I was searching for a phone among mounds of shoeboxes and toilet paper at the back, the door of the shop swung open and a voice shouted, 'HELLO, ROISÍN!'

I glanced out from behind a tower of washing powder. Oh no. It was the last person in the world I wanted to see: *Kitty*. I decided to stay hidden till she'd gone.

'ROOOOOOOISÍÍÍÍÍÍÍN!' she yelled again and this time the violin stopped.

'KITTY, KITTY, KITTY!' came a woman's voice through the floorboards. 'KITTY, KITTY, KITTY!' as she clomped down the stairs, adding, 'Kitty CAT!' as she reached the till.

'Hi, Roisín. Can I get –'

But Roisín raised a finger and interrupted. 'Oh sorry. Just one thing: can you please not chase any mice if you see one while you're in here? Or scrape your claws on any of our cardboard boxes?'

My mouth fell open. I thought this only happened to me! And I knew what was coming next: 'Hahahahahahaha!'

This is exactly where I would have gone bright red and clammed up, or just run out of the shop. But Kitty didn't. She lowered her voice, as if she was saying something really important. 'Excuse me, Roisín, I will try not to do those things, BUT –' now she got quicker and quicker – 'can I sleep on the windowsill?

'Or tear up the toilet paper?

'Or knock the cups off the shelf?

'Or get startled by my reflection in the window?

'Or cough up hairballs?

'Or bring in a dead bird?'

And then she started to jump around, making crazy cat hissing sounds: *'Meow, meow, meow!'*

This was incredible! Now they were both laughing!

Kitty continued. 'You know how much I enjoy a saucer of it, Roisín, so can I get a litre of milk, please?'

'Of course, darlin',' said Roisín.

And, when she handed it to her, Kitty said, 'That's purrfect,' and really rolled the 'r' sound. They both laughed again and Kitty meowed her way out of the shop, 'Meow, meow, meow, meow.'

Before this, if you'd asked me if it was possible for your opinion of a person to change after one conversation, I'd have said, No way. Normally, you get a first impression and that's pretty much what you think of them from then on. But my opinion of Kitty hadn't just changed – it had flipped. Now I HAD to meet her. I wanted to know how she'd figured out this way of dealing with the world, and ask her all about living on the island. And I had to find out if she knew about the strange goings-on with my uncle and her dad.

So, as soon as Roisín clomped back upstairs and the screeching violin started again, I slipped out of the door and ran after Kitty.

12

KITTY'S CASTLE

'We're going to do so many amazing things,' Kitty declared as we made our way back up the hill in the sunshine. She started counting them off on her fingers: 'Swim in the sea, go canoeing on the lake – oh, we need to build a boat first – find amethyst stones and become billionaires, ride on the back of a shark, climb to the top of the big cliff . . . I was joking about the shark.'

I wasn't so interested in some of these things, but I didn't want to interrupt.

'Wait, how long are you here? You're probably back to school on the first of September, like me, so two weeks?'

She had answered her own question, so I just nodded. I'd only said one word since we'd met, a mumbled hello.

'I'm so sorry about yesterday,' she went on. 'I just saw the sheep on the road and thought it'd be, you know, funny. But I should've known you'd be tired after your journey and, I mean, it was a very full-on thing to do to someone you've never met. But I hope we can still be friends? I promise I won't do anything like that again. Unless you want me to. Unless you're like, *Kitty, please put twelve sheep in my room* – though I don't know why you'd ask me to do that. Maybe if you were cold. Or maybe if you couldn't sleep and you'd tried counting them in your head and wanted to, you know, take it up a notch . . .'

This made me laugh.

Today Kitty was wearing a white T-shirt with **Summer** written over a picture of a rainbow. At first, I thought a rainbow was a strange image for summer. I mean, a beach maybe, or a bucket and spade, or a parasol. But the more I thought about it, the more I realized that a rainbow was the perfect image for summer in Achill.

'OK, it's time,' she said, like we'd known each other for ages and it had all been building up to this. 'I'm going to show you some things.' Then she opened a gate into a field across the road from Derm's radiator fence.

Now, as you will have realized, I am quite a cautious person, and by quite cautious I mean terrified of pretty much everything. And this was close to where I'd encountered the horrific beast-monster earlier. But something about Kitty made me want to follow her. She had a confidence, a strut – she seemed to know what she was doing. Also, I had too many questions I wanted to ask. So, when she gestured for me to come too, I stepped into the field and closed the gate behind me.

'First we have this,' she said. As we walked down towards the sea, the field stopped abruptly and gave way to a gentle cliff – no, cliff was too strong a word. It was a steep hill with a small golden beach, completely hidden from the road, at the bottom. 'This is Duncan's beach.'

'Wow!' I said. 'Does anybody else know about it?'

'Your uncle goes down there for a walk each morning. Only locals know about it. Oh, and Duncan.'

'Who's Duncan?' I asked.

'This is Duncan,' said Kitty, nodding up towards the road.

I turned round to see, trotting towards us, the beast-monster. Now I could see that it wasn't a hippo or a buffalo or whatever I'd thought it was. It was a donkey. Called Duncan.

'Are we safe?' I moved behind Kitty, which made her laugh.

'Oh, we are SO safe.' As Duncan reached us, Kitty put her hand out and rubbed his nose. 'He lives in that bush by the fence. He loves it when you rub his nose.'

'*EEEE-EEEE-EEEE-AWWW*,' said Duncan, as he danced with delight.

'Oh, he likes you,' said Kitty. Duncan was nodding excitely in my direction.

'Touch him here.' Kitty took my hand and placed it on Duncan's snout, or whatever the long part of a donkey's face with his nose at the end is called.

I went to pull away, but then . . . it actually felt quite nice. Like the bit at the back of your head when you've just had a short haircut. Duncan moved his nose back and forth so now I was stroking him.

'We'll bring you carrots next time,' said Kitty. 'Everyone loves your uncle's carrots.'

'*EEEE-AWWW EEEE-AWWW,*' agreed Duncan.

'My dad says you should talk to Duncan if you're ever down in the dumps. He always cheers you up.'

Ah! This was my chance to ask her about him. 'I met your dad this morning actually,' I said.

'Did he drop anything or almost fall over? I love him but he's very clumsy.'

'Eh, yes to both of those things,' I said. 'It was very weird because he and Derm had let off a purple smoke bomb and there was a snorkel and a drawer . . .'

'Maybe they were rehearsing a play. That's what it sounds like to me.'

'Really?' I said. I knew my uncle was interested in a lot of things, but I didn't know he liked theatre. 'But why would a play have thick purple smoke? The audience wouldn't be able to see what's going on.'

Kitty shrugged her shoulders. And, before I could ask another question, she was off. 'You won't believe the next thing!' she yelled while sprinting back up the field. Duncan and I looked at each other for a moment and then ran after her.

After a couple of hundred metres, Kitty stopped. For a moment she was standing beside what looked like a big hole in the middle of the grass, about as wide as I was tall. As I got closer, I could see that one side was a steep grassy bank leading down to stones and gravel at the bottom.

'Come on!' said Kitty. She was already halfway down and her voice echoed like she was in a great hall. I knew what my mum would have said – that I should go home, sit quietly in a chair and read a book. But Mum wasn't here.

'OK,' I said, 'I'm coming.' It was too steep for Duncan, so he waited at the top while I followed

Kitty. I spent a long time finding a safe place for each foot and hand, but soon I was descending into the hole.

'Now turn round,' said Kitty when my feet eventually touched the bottom.

'Wow!'

The hole was like a giant light bulb that lit a huge underground cavern. A gravel beach led to a pool of perfectly still water that ran out to the sea through a cave. Through the mouth of it I could see blue sky and hear distant crashing waves.

'Welcome to my castle!' said Kitty. 'I'm basically the new Grace O'Malley.'

'Who's she?' I asked.

'*Who is she?*' Kitty shook her head. She couldn't believe I didn't know. 'She's the Pirate Queen of Achill! Plundering ships that passed and giving the loot to the islanders. Some people say she used to count her money in here after a day of pirating.'

'Do they?'

'Well, I do,' she said. 'And I'm some people.'

Kitty had already begun pulling off her clothes. Underneath, she was wearing a black swimsuit with a yellow lightning bolt across the front. 'Let's get in!'

'I don't have my swimming stuff,' I said, which was technically true.

'Swim in your undies!'

I felt like I should be honest, so I said it: 'Oh, I don't.'

'You don't what?'

'I don't swim.'

'Really?' Now she was in the water up to her waist. 'But it's one of the best things.'

I shrugged my shoulders.

'There's a tube from an old car wheel over there. It's like a giant rubber ring and you could float on it.'

'No thanks,' I said.

She shook her head and dipped underwater.

For a moment, she was gone and the water went flat again. I felt a rising sense of panic, until she popped up at the opposite end of the pool.

'Rex!' she called out. 'We're going to be great friends and one day you're going to come swimming with me.'

I knew she was right about one of those things.

13

CLIMBING MOUNTAINS

'Isn't it a bit late to be doing this and, also, what are we doing?' I asked as we rode off from the house later that evening with huge bags on our backs that Kitty had packed.

'These are MOUNTAIN bikes,' she said. 'The clue is in the name.' She was riding her one, and I had put the saddle on Derm's down as low as it would go.

I'd asked Mum and Dad for a bike of my own every birthday for as long as I could remember. 'Maybe next year,' was all Mum ever said.

Kitty went on. 'We'll be up and down like that.' She took one hand off the handlebars to click her fingers and nearly rode into a ditch.

'Up and down what?' I asked nervously.

'Slievemore, of course!' she replied.

'Slieve what?' I said as I wobbled after Kitty, who had just turned off the road on to a muddy track.

She pointed up to the top of the huge mountain in front of us. 'Slievemore is basically Achill's Mount Everest, and we're going to conquer it!'

'It's a lot smaller than Mount Everest,' I said.

'Yes, it is a bit smaller,' she conceded, 'but, like Mount Everest, a lot of people have walked up it.'

'Have you?'

'I'm from here. Walking up it is a tourist thing. I want to do something that's never been done.'

'Go on.' I wasn't sure where she was going with this.

'You and I will become the first people ever to cycle up it!'

Even before I thought about it for less than half a second, it seemed like a bad idea.

'It's very steep,' I said. Already, I could feel my legs getting tired.

'Well, I have considered that,' said Kitty, 'so we'll take our time. I've planned for lots of breaks and snacks. We'll get to the top and, when the sun starts to set, then *whoosh*, we'll roll back down.' When Kitty spoke this enthusiastically, she could convince you of anything.

In retrospect, one of the main problems was our equipment. It's good to be prepared, everyone knows that, but it's also possible to be TOO prepared. Food and water, obviously, yes – but we seemed to have taken enough for a week, including a whole loaf of bread, a selection of cheeses and three two-litre bottles of water. Water, let's remember, wasn't hard to find on Achill. You just had to go outside with your mouth open and wait a few minutes.

We cycled along the track as far as we could – which wasn't very far – until it was so steep, we couldn't make the pedals turn any more.

'OK, let's walk with the bikes and get back on when it's easier,' said Kitty.

I looked up ahead. It didn't seem like it was going to get any easier.

'But does walking with our bikes still count as cycling?' I asked.

'Oh, absolutely,' said Kitty. 'It only stops being cycling if you're not touching the bike.'

There was a pause while I thought about this.

'But then, when you're learning to ride, you're cycling even if you're just walking along with your bike?'

'We should probably talk less,' said Kitty. 'Conserve our energy.'

Twenty minutes of no talking later, our breath was getting louder and my arms and legs were starting to ache. We were still a very long way from the top.

'OK, new plan,' said Kitty. 'Let's leave the bikes here by this spiky bush and walk the rest of the way.'

'But I thought we were cycling to the –'

'Sometimes the mark of a great plan is that it changes midway through.' She said it like it was a famous phrase that everyone knew. I didn't object.

Kitty walked in front while I trailed behind.

'How close to the top are we?' I asked after we'd been going for ages.

'Let me check the map,' said Kitty. She rummaged around in her backpack and pulled out a hardback book of maps. 'Now, we are . . . Where are we?' She was moving the map book round in a circle as if she was driving a bus. I looked at my watch. It was 9.30 p.m. already and the light was starting to fade.

'Can I help?' I asked after a minute.

'No, no. I've nearly got it,' she said, cross-referencing the map with the compass she had on a string round her neck.

I looked at the cover of the book. **MAPS OF ICELAND** it said in big letters.

'Eh, Kitty?'

'Give me one more second,' she said, leafing through a few more pages.

'That's, eh, well . . .' I didn't want to sound rude. 'They're not the right maps.'

She checked the front and slammed the book shut. 'It's very close to *Maps of Ireland*,' she said. 'Just one letter away.' As if the maps should therefore be similar too.

It stays brighter later on Achill, but when it gets dark it does so really quickly. On a night like this, when the clouds covered the moon, soon we couldn't see a thing.

'Kitty, we should use the torch now,' I said. 'We could easily step into a hole or twist an ankle.'

'You worry too much,' said Kitty. 'Also, we don't want to waste the batteries. We might need it in an emergen–' She tripped over a small rock that was sticking out of the ground. I helped her up, but I could tell she'd hurt her toe.

'OK, where's the torch?' I said.

'Listen –' Kitty was quite flustered now – 'I had to make certain packing decisions earlier, based on each item's usefulness and weight.'

'You brought a garden gnome,' I said. I could see his head sticking out of her bag.

'The plan was to take a photo with him at the top!'

'Did you forget the camera, though?'

'Yes, I did,' said Kitty.

'And did you maybe forget the torch?'

'Yes.'

There was a moment where we both stood facing each other. At least, I think we did. It was very dark. Then I said it. 'We should go back now.'

'No way,' said Kitty. 'The plan is that we go to the top.'

'Kitty, you don't climb mountains in the dark. It's too dangerous.'

'But that's not the plan,' she said, becoming more agitated.

'Sometimes,' I began, like it was a saying that had been in my family for generations, 'the mark of a great plan is that it changes midway through.'

Kitty turned away because she knew she couldn't win. But she had one more idea. 'I've got a tent. How about we put it up here, and then walk the rest of the way when it gets light?'

'But Derm and your dad won't know where we are,' I said.

'Derm gave me the tent when I told him the plan,' Kitty said.

I couldn't argue with that.

Tents are difficult to put up, I think we can all agree. Old tents, like the one Derm had given Kitty, are even trickier. And putting up an old tent with no instructions in the dark when you're tired is almost impossible. Forgetting the torch was especially surprising as, in the course of unpacking the tent from her bag, I saw that Kitty had managed to bring a tennis racket (in case we needed to chase sheep away), a jigsaw (in case we got bored) and a dressing gown (I have no idea).

Some tents are dome-shaped; some are, well, tent-shaped. After thirty minutes of construction, ours was shaped like a pyramid, and soon we were lying end to end in our sleeping bags along different sides of it.

'I think Derm and Ronan are planning something,' I said to Kitty, 'but I've no idea what.'

'It's probably nothing,' said Kitty. 'There are a lot of things Derm wants to do before . . .' She trailed off.

'Before what?' I asked. 'Before the end of the summer?'

'Yeah,' said Kitty in a sleepy voice that soon turned into long, sleepy breaths and then tiny, breathy snores.

I was tired too, but lying halfway up a mountain in a rickety tent, with somebody I had only met properly that morning, I realized that Derm had been right about one thing: I did enjoy being out of my comfort zone.

14

THE DELUGE

It started like the sound of a distant radio – one not tuned to any station. But it couldn't have been a radio because Kitty and I were alone on a mountainside, with only sheep around us. And sheep don't listen to the radio.

Then it got louder.

Uh-oh. My suspicions were confirmed when the first drop fell on my sleeping bag. From being a perfectly fine night ten minutes before, it was now raining the sort of rain that only falls in the jungle at certain times of year or when you're in a tent on a mountain on an island that sticks out into the Atlantic Ocean.

I didn't then and still don't know much about tents, but I knew that they're supposed to have a waterproof outer sheet and that we hadn't put one up. We'd been so tired when we were setting it up that it hadn't occurred to me.

Soon the rain turned from single droplets into streams, pouring in on top of us.

'Kitty. Kitty! KITTY!' I shouted.

She sat bolt upright and in a still-dreaming voice said, 'I'm the Pirate Queen!' before shaking the rain off her face.

'Where's the waterproof sheet?' I asked, frantically unzipping the bags around me.

'It was too heavy!'

'Heavy?' I said. 'You brought your clarinet!'

'I know, I know. I've made some mistakes.' For the first time in the twelve hours I'd known her, I detected a note of panic in Kitty's voice.

'Not to worry,' I said in the most positive tone I could muster. 'We'll leave all this here and cycle home now. We can come back and get it tomorrow.'

She nodded. 'OK.'

The rain was so heavy that the moment we stepped outside we were soaked.

'Well, at least we can't get any wetter,' I said. But I was wrong.

Just as the rain on Achill was somehow wetter than any rain I'd ever known, the darkness was darker.

'Can I hold your hand?' Kitty asked.

'Of course,' I said.

There was nothing to guide us except gravity and our bums when we slipped on the wet grass and mud. But they were enough to lead us back to the bikes. We walked them down to the road, and set off home at the slowest pace bicycles can go without falling over.

There wasn't a single car, but still a journey that had taken twenty minutes earlier now took almost two hours. A strange thing happens when you're completely soaked and more tired than you've ever been and your clothes weigh so much you think it might be easier just to take them off and cycle in your undies. The slightest things become hilarious: Kitty baaing at sheep and them baaing back; the squealing sound your brakes make in the wet; the thought of how bizarre we must have looked to anyone who happened to peer out of their window to see two mud-soaked children out for a cycle in the middle of the night. We reached Derm's gate at 1 a.m.

I was surprised to see Ronan's car still parked by the gate, but it gave Kitty an idea.

'We basically look like monsters, so let's give Dad and Derm a fright!'

I laughed hysterically at the idea. This was exactly the sort of thing Derm would love.

We rolled the bikes up the driveway and peered in through the window to see them still sitting at the table, taking turns to move a salt cellar around a large map of the island. Apart from the dim lamp on the table between them, all the other lights in the house were off.

Kitty held a finger to her lips and we crept round to the back door. She slid the handle open, and I went in first. As I crept forward in the shadows of the kitchen, I could hear their conversation.

'When the last customer has left, then, bang, you throw the smoke bomb in,' Derm said.

Ronan nodded. 'Then I count to one hundred . . .'

'No, you count to ten. One hundred is too much.'

'OK, and then I grab the drawer and run out.'

'And I'll be driving past with the back doors of the van open.'

I'd never heard my uncle talk like this before. He sounded so serious. It must have been the play Kitty had mentioned.

'What about traffic?' asked Ronan. 'What if we get stuck behind the bus?' His hand moved across the map, knocking over the salt cellar, which temporarily covered Slievemore in a layer of salty snow.

'I think that's definitely a risk,' said Derm. 'But there are always risks when you rob a bank.'

If my eyes could have shot out of my head on stalks, like they do in cartoons, they would have. This wasn't a play.

Kitty suddenly cleared her throat, which made Derm and Ronan spin round. There was total silence till Kitty said, 'Surprise!'

A look of shock came over Ronan and Derm that must have been similar to the look of shock on my face.

'*Rob a bank?*' The words were out of my mouth before I could stop them.

'Ray!' Ronan babbled. 'It's not . . . We're not really going to . . .'

Derm stood up slowly. 'Oh, T-Rex, I didn't want you to find out. But now you know, so we definitely can't. It's off.'

'Not that we were actually going to do it,' said Ronan.

'Come on,' Derm said to him. 'It's time to be honest.'

Ronan nodded. 'When Kitty found out, that was only one person, but two is too many.'

I looked at Kitty. 'Wait, you knew?'

For once, Kitty didn't say anything. She kept looking over at the fridge.

'That's why you've been avoiding my questions!'

Kitty still didn't say anything, but I saw her eyes fill with tears.

'Goodnight.' I turned and headed straight for the big Spanish ice cream, then bolted my bedroom door behind me.

15

TOO MUCH INFORMATION

One good thing about travelling light is that it doesn't take long to pack. I bundled everything into my small blue backpack and, as soon as it was bright, climbed out of the window and ran down the driveway, turning left past Kitty's house, and down the hill to the bus stop.

At 9.02 a.m. the bus to Westport train station pulled out, and I found myself sitting beside an old lady who wanted to know EVERYTHING about me.

I thought about pretending to be French and not understanding, but there was the risk that she could actually speak French and would start speaking French back to me.

'I'm Saoirse. What's your name?' she asked.

I decided to try to shut the conversation down by giving the most boring possible answers.

'Alan,' I said. (It was a toss-up between Alan and David.)

What was I doing on the island?

Holidays.

Why was I going home on my own?

The car was full.

Why?

That's the problem with lying. In no time, you end up getting tangled in knots. Why was I going home on my own? Why was the car full? Had my family somehow got bigger on holiday? Or maybe the car had shrunk in the rain?

I tried to think what Kitty would say. She would be imaginative.

'The dog jumps around a lot,' I said. Not bad, but it needed a little more. 'And pees on you.' From the reaction on Saoirse's face, I knew I'd gone too far. Also, it opened the door to so many more questions.

How old was the dog?

Seven.

What breed?

Mix.

Did it chase sheep?

Yes, but in quite a friendly way.

Before she could ask any more questions, Saoirse was distracted by a sign at the side of the road.

THE RECENT ACT OF VANDALISM HAS BEEN REPAIRED AND THE BRIDGE HAS REOPENED

She had a lot to say about it. 'Whoever opened that bridge should be ashamed of themselves and so should anyone who knows anything about it. I mean, it's the only way on and off the island – especially during the busiest time of the year. Why would anybody do that?'

'I don't know,' I said. And I genuinely didn't.

*

I was glad when Saoirse got off just after the bridge because it gave me some time to think.

Leaving had been dramatic – but not as dramatic as robbing a bank. Why would Derm take a risk like that? I knew that my uncle had done things in the past that were slightly illegal – letting me drive his van on the beach, for example. But robbing a bank? That's what bad people did. You could go to prison for robbing a bank.

I felt angry at Kitty too. Yes, I'd just met her, but it had felt so intense. How could she not have told me? A real friend would never keep a secret like that.

Back in Westport train station, I checked the timetable. There were still two hours till the next train to Dublin. I bought a student ticket with the money Derm had given me and sat on a bench.

Finally, at 12.20 the train arrived and about a hundred people got off. Some were carrying fishing rods, some pushed bikes. Most looked like they were going to Achill for the festival. I was happy to be getting away from it. I sat in the back row of the last carriage, as far from everyone else as I could get.

I decided that I'd go straight to the hospital and give Mum a surprise. I still hadn't phoned, but it would give her a shock if I did now. I wouldn't mention the robbery. I'd tell her Derm had been too busy and I had decided to come home. She'd be in for another week and a half, so I'd stay with boring Aunt Fiona and the perfect twins. No doubt they'd be busy winning trophies at karate or archery or whatever new thing they were brilliant at.

Soon she'd be home and things would get back to normal. Or new normal. Without Dad.

Soon I wasn't alone in the carriage any more. People had started boarding through the door behind me. It was mostly families, probably going home after their holidays, then a few older people maybe on a trip to Dublin. Then a tall girl with a wonky plait . . . Wait!

'Kitty!' I blurted, and she spun round and jumped into the empty seat beside me.

She grabbed my hands and spoke in intense bursts. 'I'm so sorry I didn't tell you about it. I should have! They didn't mean to tell me, but you know what my dad's like. He kept dropping maps and bits of paper with their plans on them. I promised I wouldn't tell anyone, but I should have made an exception for you, Rex . . . I'm just so sorry.'

A crackling voice came over the loudspeaker. 'This train is departing in two minutes, thank you.'

'What are you doing here? You're not coming to Dublin, are you?' I asked.

She shook her head. 'I called by to apologize earlier, and when I saw your bedroom window was open . . . I guessed you'd be here – it's what I would have done.'

I was distracted for a moment. 'What's that weird smell?'

'Oh sorry, it's me. I hitched a ride with my cousin in his stinky fish truck.'

'Kitty, what they're planning is dangerous. But the main thing is that it's just wrong. Wrong, wrong, wrong.'

'I know,' said Kitty, 'but . . .'

'But what?' I said. 'There is no "but".'

She looked down at the floor. 'There's something you need to know.'

'What?' I said.

'Derm isn't well.'

'Isn't well what?'

'No, I mean he's sick.'

'No, he *was* sick,' I said. 'He was in hospital and he got better.'

She shook her head. 'It's come back.'

'WHAT?' Suddenly it felt like there was ringing in my ears and my eyes were starting to blur. 'Wait, how do you know?'

'I heard him tell Dad.'

'You must have heard it wrong.'

Kitty shook her head again. 'He was telling Dad what he wants to happen to his ashes.'

The loudspeaker came on again. 'We are departing in one minute.'

This was too much information to take in. 'I have to talk to him,' I said.

The inspector appeared at the front of the carriage. 'Everybody who is not travelling, please disembark now.'

I grabbed my backpack and we jumped off together.

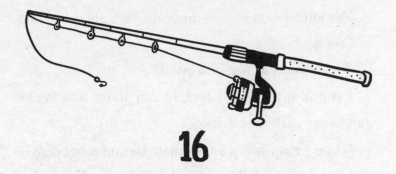

16

GOING FOR DINNER

'You have to flick your wrist,' said Derm that evening as we stood on the flat rock beside Duncan's beach. Kitty and I had just made the last bus back to the island. When my uncle said we should go out for dinner, I assumed we'd be going to a restaurant so we could talk. But no. Derm meant stand on a rock with a fishing rod and try to catch our dinner.

'You're holding the rod too tight. Hold it like it's a small bird.'

'I've never held a small bird,' I said.

'A mouse?'

'Yuck.'

'How about a frog or a snail?'

I shook my head. 'I feel, in our lives, that we've held very different things.'

'Then imagine it's a chocolate bar on a hot day.'

I finally got what he meant, but the truth was that after the twenty-four hours I'd had, the last thing I wanted was to catch a fish.

It was a calm evening, but inside my head questions were clanging off each other.

'I understand why you left,' Derm said, answering the first one. 'And I'm so sorry. It was such a stupid plan and, I promise you, we're not doing it now.'

'Kitty told me everything,' I said. 'Why didn't you tell me?'

'Well, I suppose we were so wrapped up in the planning –'

I interrupted. 'No, not the robbery.'

'What?'

'Why didn't you tell me that you're . . . dying.' The moment I said it, I instantly regretted it.

But Derm didn't mind. He turned with a wide smile across his face. 'I didn't tell you because it's so boring. I mean, if you think about it, we're all dying. You are, your mum is, Duncan the donkey is. For some people, it'll take ages. For others, it could happen today.'

'You still could have –' I tried to interrupt, but Derm wasn't finished.

'T-Rex, at the same time that we're dying, do you know what else we're all doing?'

I was about to say fishing, but Derm answered his own question.

'Living! And that's what I've tried to put all my energy into. To squeeze every drop out of each day. To surround myself with the best things –' he pointed at the scenery around us – 'and the best people.' He pointed at me. 'And try to have the best life! Some people live to be a hundred and never have any of this.' He cast his hook out again. 'I feel so lucky!'

I looked down and noticed wet blobs on my red sweatshirt, but this time it hadn't been raining. 'Why were you going to rob a bank?'

There was a pause while Derm wound his hook in. 'You remember Angley?'

'The red, angry man?' I said.

Derm nodded. 'He owns all the hotels on the island and he wants to open another, where the Old Coastguard Station is now.'

'But what about the people who live there?' I said.

'He doesn't care about them. He only cares about getting it shut down. For this, he needs to have the building declared unsafe. So he keeps trying to bring the building inspector over from Dublin. I've been doing my best to make sure he doesn't get here.'

'Is that why you changed the direction of the signs?'

Derm nodded.

'And why we opened the bridge?'

Derm nodded again. It made sense now.

He continued. 'That building needs a lot of work and will cost big money to fix up. But, if we can get it done before the inspector gets here, he can't shut it down, and the people who live there can stay.

And then, when the time comes –' he shrugged his shoulders – 'I can go there too.'

This was a lot to take in. 'There must be another option,' I said. 'An easier way to get money.'

'We've written to all the politicians and sent petitions, but they tell us they have no money for the island.'

'Oh, come on!' I said. I was quite angry now.

'Do you know how to raise a lot of money?' Derm asked.

I thought for a moment. 'I might have an idea,' I said.

'Let's talk about it while we eat. I'm afraid it's just veggies tonight.'

But, as I wound my line in, the tip of my rod began to twitch like a scratchy finger.

'Oh no!' I said, and handed it over to Derm.

He beamed. 'You weren't holding it too tight, T-Rex! Fish is back on the menu.'

17

BOUNCYLAND

'Roll up, roll up!' shouted Kitty over the heads of the hundreds of tourists and locals who had gathered on the grass across the road from the Old Coastguard Station. 'Welcome to the Old Coastguard Station Fundraising Day!'

'You should be very proud of yourself,' Derm said to me. But it wasn't really my idea. When Mum and Dad were still together, they'd organized one for the school. People came along because they wanted to show how much they loved it. Well, it turned out that people loved the Old Coastguard Station even more.

Besides, Derm had done most of the work. He'd spent the day before on Roisín's payphone, calling in favours from everyone he could think of. This was while Kitty and I made posters and cycled round the island, sticking them everywhere.

Ingenious stalls and attractions vied for attention and donations.

Malcolm, the goalkeeper for the Achill Rovers football team, stood in the middle of a goal. You paid 50 cents to take a penalty. Score, and you won a euro. It was 2 p.m. and nobody had scored yet.

Across from him, Ronan was in charge of one of the most popular attractions: sheep racing. Six sheep with different-coloured paint blotches on their coats waited in a pen, and you bet on which one you thought would cross the finishing line first. The races took a long time because the sheep were much more interested in eating all the tasty grass on the way than getting to the finish line.

Boom-Boom, Derm's friend who worked as the explosives expert in a quarry, had taken over a whole field. He let you blow things up you hated for three euro. Irene from the Post Office had just quit smoking and blew up her last pack of cigarettes. Roisín blew up the computer someone had given her to help organize her shop.

Kitty and I were in charge of Bouncyland, where it was 20 cents for ten minutes of bouncing on some of Derm's large inflatable things we had dragged from his shed. Kitty's job was to pull in a crowd and mine was to connect the air hose from the air compressor to whichever bouncy thing needed more air.

There was a huge inflatable book that had once been attached to the front of a library, and beside it a massive ring doughnut. The problem with the doughnut was that, at first, people kept falling into the hole. We solved this by wedging a large inflatable car into the centre of it.

'We are full of good ideas!' said Kitty.

'Alan, Alan!' a vaguely familiar voice called over at one point. It was Saoirse from the bus. 'You decided to come back!'

'Oh yes,' I said, trying to think of a reason why. 'I didn't want to miss this!'

'We all love the Old Coastguard Station,' she said, adding, 'I hope your dog has stopped peeing on you,' and wandered off, leaving Kitty very confused.

As Derm walked through the crowd, I realized how much everybody loved him. In the time he'd lived here, he seemed to have fixed something for every person on the island.

Not everyone was happy, though. Sergeant Crummey, Achill's only police officer, was furious that he hadn't been notified about the event. He was running around, frantically warning anyone who would listen about health-and-safety breaches.

'See that inflatable doughnut?' he said to Kitty at one point. 'What if it springs a leak like a giant balloon and shoots out to sea with little children hanging from it?'

Sergeant Crummey was not the brightest member of the police force, which must have been why they'd put him on an island where there was virtually no crime. Still, he took his job VERY seriously.

'This isn't dangerous!' Kitty said. 'But over there I can see something that is.'

Crummey whirled round and saw a helicopter hovering over the crowd. People had to rush out of the way as it came in to land in front of the Old Coastguard Station. When it had touched down, two figures stepped out, one in a grey suit and the other I identified from the red flap of hair bouncing on the top of his head as Angley. Five minutes later, the grey-suited man had walked round the building once and got back into the helicopter. Angley began hammering a sign into the ground. He spotted Derm and shouted over, 'Lovely day for whatever this is, Dermot! And it'll be even lovelier in thirty days' time because the building inspector has just assessed it and that's when we can start knocking this dump down!'

'What about the people that live there, Mr Angley?' Derm shouted back. 'Where are they supposed to go?'

'Maybe they should have thought about that before they got sick!' He hit the sign a few more times, adding, 'You'll need a miracle to save it now!'

To emphasize his point, he went to give one big final whack, but missed the sign and struck himself on the foot. This caused him to collapse on to the ground and roll around in great pain, till the man in the grey suit got back out and helped him into the helicopter.

Derm shouted over, 'If you need medical help, there's a place just behind you!'

As the helicopter took off, Crummey, who had gone back to his car to get a notebook, finally arrived on the scene. 'Make way for a police officer . . . oh, I've missed it,' he said. 'Can somebody give me a description of the helicopter?' he asked, but everyone ignored him.

It had been a hugely successful day, but Derm was silent as we drove back up to the house.

'What does "condemned" mean?' Kitty asked. 'It's written on Angley's sign.'

'It's not good,' I said. 'It means it's dangerous and they can knock it down.'

'Why did he say "in thirty days"?'

Ronan explained. 'By law, they have to give you some time to fix it up.'

'Well, let's fix it up!' said Kitty. 'Derm will know what to do and loads of people will help.'

Derm smiled. 'It needs a new roof, and new walls, and it's damp underneath. It will cost a lot in materials.'

'How much?' Kitty asked.

'Over a hundred thousand.'

'And how much did we raise today?' she asked.

'About two thousand,' said Derm.

'Not bad,' said Kitty. 'By my calculations, we just need to put on another forty-nine of these in the next month!'

Derm didn't laugh.

'We are going to think of something, Rex, aren't we?' she said.

I nodded, even if I wasn't sure we were.

*

Kitty and I were sitting in front of Derm's house later in the evening when we saw a car with a plume of black smoke coming from its exhaust pipe drive up the hill. The setting sun reflected off the windscreen until it was close by and I could see the grinning red face of Angley, who was sitting in the passenger seat, holding a pair of crutches. For a moment, I thought his conscience might have got to him. But I was wrong.

'Where's your dad?' he barked through the passenger window.

I didn't bother correcting him. 'He's tired and went to bed early.'

Two men jumped out of the car and went over to the side of Derm's van.

'What's going on?' Kitty demanded.

'Tell him I've returned the maple syrup he put into my petrol tank the other night. The garage were able to get most of it out, but make sure you thank him because otherwise I wouldn't have got to go in that helicopter.'

One of his henchmen had removed Derm's petrol cap while the other was pouring in a brown substance from a large fuel can.

'You can't do that!' said Kitty, and charged towards them. The bigger one laughed and pushed her to the ground. I felt a surge of anger.

'NEVER push my friend!' I said, and attempted my first-ever and, I would imagine, only-ever rugby tackle. The big man swatted me to the gravel and laughed.

'You kids will enjoy my new hotel,' Angley said as they got back into his car. 'It's going to have a pool. Oh no, wait. You're both barred.'

I went over to help Kitty up. Our hands stayed clasped together as we watched the car go back down the driveway.

'We can't let him get away with this,' said Kitty. 'We have to think of something.'

I nodded. 'Yes, we do.'

18

DIGGING FOR TREASURE

I pushed open my bedroom door and shuffled out into the sun-filled kitchen. I'd never slept that long before.

'That's the sea air, T-Rex!' Derm called out from his bedroom when he heard my footsteps. 'It really knocks you out.'

'Hi,' I said, shielding my eyes from the brightness. I usually had more to say than 'hi', but after a long sleep it sometimes takes a while for my brain to wake up.

I put my head round his door. My uncle was lying in bed with towers of books piled around him.

'I always used to be the first up. But things take a bit longer these days,' he said.

On the wall were photographs of family and friends – there was one of him and Mum as kids, one of me when I was nine, flying a kite he'd made. To the side, a couch functioned as a wardrobe for his clothes, and under the window, his desk was three-quarters covered in a mountain of torn-out articles from newspapers and magazines and filed in a system that would have made my mother scream. In contrast, the last part of the desk was arranged in neat lines of pill jars and packets of tablets, all underneath a calendar listing what to take on which day.

Derm noticed me staring at it. 'See, your uncle can be very organized when he needs to be.'

'Angley called last night when you were asleep,' I said. 'Did you put maple syrup into his car the other night?'

'He didn't come back and put some in my van, did he?'

I nodded.

Derm shrugged his shoulders. 'My van won't mind that. It'll be like a treat for it!'

Just as I turned to go back to the kitchen, he made a sound like the door of a haunted castle. '*UUUUUUUUUUUUUGH. T-Rex! Just . . . one . . . more . . . thing!*'

I peered slowly back round the door. He had draped one hand dramatically over his forehead while still holding the book he was reading with the other.

'I think I might pass out if I don't have a *c-c-cup of tea* –' here his voice began to quiver like these could be his final words – '*in my orange teapot – and just two eggs – scrambled – on a bit of toast – no, wait, two bits . . . And some butter on the side . . . please?*'

I stared at him for a moment, then smiled. 'Yes, Your Majesty.' And set to work.

I had just given Derm his breakfast when Kitty burst into the kitchen.

'Come on. I've got a plan!'

Moments later, we were both cycling down the road, wobbling a little because Kitty had tied shovels to our crossbars.

'We're going to dig for treasure!' she shouted across to me. 'There's definitely buried pirate loot on the island.'

This sounded interesting. 'Did you find an old map or something?' I asked.

'No, but I had an idea: if we try to imagine we are pirates, like try really, really hard, and then ask ourselves, "*Where would we bury our treasure?*"'

I waited for her to go on, but that was it.

It had all the hallmarks of a Kitty plan. A strong initial idea, but then no detail. That said, it was the only plan we had at that moment.

'Short cut here!' she yelled, and we turned left at a fork in the road. We wound our way through a tunnel of trees until suddenly everything disappeared. Well, not everything, but there were no houses or pubs or shops – not even any fields. Just the narrow ribbon of raised road we were cycling along and a drop down to a boggy marsh on either side. It was the kind of landscape you think of when you imagine where dinosaurs lived millions of years ago. But, instead of swooping pterodactyls or galloping raptors, there were just a few sheep dotted around the place, munching disinterestedly on whatever grass they could find.

'Where's everything gone?' I asked.

'This is the Bog Road,' said Kitty. 'It's the quickest way across the middle of the island, but not much happens in the middle of the island so nobody comes this way. All the action is around the edges, like . . . like the opposite of a pizza.' I understood what she meant.

We'd been cycling along the road for five or six minutes and not seen a single car when suddenly – *BANG!* Kitty went over something pointy and it blew a hole in her tyre. The bike wouldn't ride with a puncture, so our treasure-hunting mission was cancelled and we started to walk home.

'I still haven't phoned my mum,' I said.

'Oh, I should phone mine too,' said Kitty.

'Why do you need to phone your mum?'

'She lives in London.'

'Really?'

'Rex, so do I.'

'What?'

She nodded. 'I grew up here, but now I just come back for all the school holidays to be with my dad.'

'I had no idea. Does your mum miss your dad?' I asked.

'Oh no, she doesn't miss him at all. They divorced when I was eight. She's married to Nish now and I have two new brothers.'

I hadn't expected any of this and must have had a surprised expression on my face because Kitty said, 'You know, it's not particularly unusual.'

'What's it like?'

'What do you mean?'

And then I said it for the first time. 'My parents have just broken up.' I waited for something to happen. For hailstones to fall or for the ground to shake. But everything stayed exactly the same.

'Aw, I'm sorry,' said Kitty. 'It's really hard to begin with, but I promise it's fine after a while. It's better actually because, well, mine used to argue all the time. They're much happier now.'

It took a moment for all this to sink in. It had seemed impossible that I could ever feel OK again, but maybe I would.

Still no traffic had passed so we were walking our bikes down the middle of the road. I heard a distant sound that I presumed was a sheep, but then we both heard it again and turned to see the mobile bank van speeding towards us as it beeped its horn. There wasn't enough room for it to pass and there wasn't enough time for us to safely move off the road, so we both had to fling our bikes to the side and jump. We looked up from the damp marsh in time to see Pointy and Driver laughing as they zoomed by.

'Nobody likes them,' said Kitty as she helped me back to my feet. 'They're always mean.'

'They were mean to me on my first day,' I said.

'Doesn't surprise me.'

'I wonder what would have happened if Ronan and Derm had gone ahead with their plan?' I said.

'Knowing my dad, he'd have grabbed the wrong drawer and come back with a bunch of leaflets.'

'Where were they going to do it?'

'By the bus stop, outside Roisín's, I think.'

'Too risky.' I shook my head. 'It's far too busy there. Also, that smoke bomb would have attracted too much attention. When were they going to do it?'

'Some time in the next few months, when it gets dark earlier, I think.'

'No, no, no,' I said. 'That's a mistake. You should do it when the most money is onboard.'

'You really sound like you know what you're talking about,' Kitty said.

I was surprised too. I suppose, after a lifetime of worrying too much about everything, I was very good at spotting the best ways to avoid danger.

'When does the festival end?' I asked.

'The closing parade is on Monday.'

'Well, Monday would be the day to rob it,' I said.

'How would you do it?' Kitty asked.

'I'd make them stop in the middle of nowhere, but I'd do it in a completely different way.'

'How?'

'Well, firstly, I wouldn't. That money belongs to other people – people who live and work on the island.'

'It doesn't,' said Kitty. 'Or at least it doesn't after the bank teller stamps the deposit form. Then they're in charge of it. If it's stolen, the bank has to pay you back. Also, it's a bank and they have gazillions.'

'Well, it's still stealing, and stealing is wrong.'

'Yeah, stealing is bad,' said Kitty, 'but . . .'

'But what?'

'But what if *not* stealing is worse?'

'What do you mean?'

'Like if you take somebody's bike, that's bad. But, if you've just been bitten by a snake and you only have fifteen minutes to get to the hospital, would it be OK to steal a bike then?'

'No, I mean, yeah, but . . .'

She went on. 'Grace O'Malley used to steal from passing ships and give it to the people of the island.'

'That was plundering,' I said.

'Plundering is stealing!'

I thought about it for a moment. 'Maybe,' I said. 'Maybe.'

19

A PERFECT CRIME

'It really is so quiet driving this bank van along at –'
I removed one hand from the invisible steering wheel
and checked the clock on the imaginary dashboard –
'two p.m. in the afternoon approximately.'

It was after dinner on Sunday. Kitty and I had
been rehearsing in Derm's shed for a day and a half.
We hadn't told Ronan and Derm what it was about,
just that we'd written a theatrical piece that we'd
like to perform for them. All the blinds in Derm's
kitchen were closed and we were both squashed
together side by side on the same chair in the
middle of the floor.

'Yes, Driver, it is quiet. But it's always quiet out here on the Bog Road,' Kitty said, in her version of the pointy-faced bank teller's voice. Her drawn-on moustache moved up and down as she spoke. 'Whoa, slow down! Look at all those sheep on the road up ahead.'

Here I stood up, removed my hat and spoke in my normal voice. 'You see, we've got sheep to block the road by putting a bunch of Derm's carrots in the middle of it.' I put the hat back on, sat down and said gruffly, 'We can't drive on with all these sheep in the way!'

'I'll get out and move them,' said Kitty, again in her Pointy voice. She mimed climbing out of the door of the van and then hooshing the invisible sheep away, accompanying herself with a few quiet baas. Even if Ronan and Derm didn't like our plan, they could still enjoy some pretty good acting.

I explained what would happen next: 'So, you two have been hiding on either side of the road. Now there's a chance they'll both get out to move the sheep, in which case – perfect – you jump into the van, one each side. If only one gets out, you both get in that side, and your first job is to push the other person out. Then you lock the doors.'

Kitty wiped her moustache off with her sleeve to show that she was no longer Pointy, and demonstrated pushing me off the chair. 'It won't be too hard, as it's the last thing they'll be expecting in the middle of the Bog Road. Then you drive off.'

Ronan raised his hand.

'Yes, question from Ronan,' Kitty said, like she was a teacher.

'When do I throw the smoke bomb?'

'Zero smoke bombs, Dad, I'm afraid. Zero snorkels too.'

'Oh, I see.' You could tell he was quite disappointed.

'We're not just taking the money any more,' I explained. 'We're taking the whole van.'

'But that's a lot more complicated,' said Derm.

'In a way, yes,' I said, 'but too many things can go wrong if you're trying to snatch the money and run. What if the teller grabs it before Ronan does? Or what if he grabs Ronan and locks the door of the bank? What if your van decides not to start?'

Ronan put his hand up again.

'Yes, Ronan,' I said.

'But won't they be able to see who we are?'

'Good question,' I began. 'Hopefully, they won't see you, but, if they do, you'll be in disguise. We found these old suits in Derm's shed – a brown one for Pointy – that's you, Ronan – and this blue one with a blue cap for you, Derm. You're Driver.'

Kitty held up the suits. We'd glued silver paper to the shoulders of Derm's one and the front of his cap to make him look more – well, I'm not sure why we'd done that. It was Kitty's idea.

She continued. 'The driver has a beard and the teller has a moustache, so you can draw them on with this burnt cork.' She demonstrated this by rubbing it across my face, leaving me with a black squiggly beard. 'You should consider keeping that,' she added.

'I'll think about it,' I said.

We sat back down on the chair and pretended to be in the van again. 'So now,' I explained, 'you both drive off, leaving the real driver and the bank teller in the middle of the Bog Road. By my estimate, it will take them at least thirty minutes to walk to the nearest house to raise the alarm. But instead of taking the van up some back road and then abandoning it when you've got the money –'

Kitty jumped in here: 'Which could leave fingerprints and clues everywhere.'

'You'll continue along the road back here.' I pointed towards the end of the driveway. 'When you get to the gate, you'll check to see there are no cars. And then you drive it up here. Kitty and I will be waiting with the doors of the shed open.'

'But then we'll be stuck with the van forever!' said Ronan.

'No,' I said. 'After we've got the money out, we wait till it gets dark, then use the digger to bury it under Derm's vegetable patch.'

'Nobody ever sees it again,' said Kitty.

'It vanishes,' I added.

'Wow!' said Ronan, clapping his hands. He was impressed. 'Kitty and Ray, that's close to a perfect crime.' He looked over at Derm, who wasn't giving much away. 'Derm,' Ronan went on, 'we could practise it a few times till we get it perfect.'

'Ah,' I said. 'That's the other thing. There are no practices. If we're going to do this, it has to be tomorrow.'

'WHAT!' said Ronan.

I continued. 'It's the end of the Summer Festival and the biggest day of the year for the bank.'

'But tomorrow's too soon!' said Ronan.

'Dad,' Kitty said. 'If we want to save the Old Coastguard Station, tomorrow is our only chance.'

There was silence in the kitchen. Derm was staring down at the tiles. Then he spoke. 'You can't be part of it. That's the rule. We'll get the van into the shed and bury it ourselves. You both have to go off somewhere for the day. Otherwise you'll be accessories. Do you know what that means?'

'Like a matching hat and scarf?' Kitty suggested with a smile on her face.

'No,' said Derm. For once, he wasn't in the mood for jokes. 'It means I don't want to have to phone

Rex's mother and say, "Oh, I hope your leg is feeling better and by the way your son's in prison."'

Kitty nodded. 'We're just kids. We don't know anything.'

Derm took a deep breath. 'OK.' He turned to look at Ronan, and Ronan nodded back at him. 'We'll do it.'

20

THE MORNING
OF THE DAY

I finally telephoned Mum. It was the morning of the robbery and I thought I should, in case the next time I spoke to her . . . Well, we don't need to go into that.

'Sorry I haven't been in touch,' I said. 'Derm doesn't have a phone and it's been very busy.'

Mum was curious. 'What have you been doing, Rexypoos?'

I tried to think of something I'd done that wouldn't horrify her, but it was difficult. Cycling up a mountain at night? *No.* Going out in a boat and seeing a shark? *No way*. Planning a bank robbery? *DEFINITELY NOT.*

'I met a new friend called Kitty,' I said.

'And what does she like to do?' Mum asked.

'She loves to swim,' I said without thinking, and that was a huge mistake.

'Oh no, Rex. No, no, no. I hope there's a lifeguard at the pool where she goes.'

'She swims in the sea, Mum,' I said. And that really started her off.

'No, no, no,' she kept saying. 'How many times have I warned you about people like that? Stay away from her. You don't like the sea! All the rocks and the waves? And you're so small. What if there's a storm and it washes my little Rexypoos out to sea with all the sharkies?'

'They don't have proper teeth, Mum.'

She ignored that. 'This girl sounds like a bad influence.'

The phone beeped. 'Mum, my money's nearly gone and I don't have any more coins so I hope you're feeling bett–' The line went dead.

I walked over to where Kitty was minding our bikes.

'How's your mum?' she asked.

'Same as usual,' I said, and we cycled back up the hill to Derm's.

Ronan and Derm had arranged to meet at 10 a.m., but Ronan overslept and had to be woken by Kitty, so it was closer to 11 when he arrived up at Derm's with sweat dripping down his forehead. For the first time since I'd been on the island, the sky was pure blue. It was the hottest day of the year.

I made them toast and tea while Kitty put together some emergency cheese sandwiches they could take with them. Derm and Ronan's conversation didn't sound like one that master criminals usually have before a heist, but at least they weren't mumbling to each other any more.

'Do we have to walk all the way?' Ronan asked.

'Yes,' Derm said. 'If we drive and the police find our car, they'll know who did it.'

Ronan wasn't finished. 'Why do we have to carry our disguises? Why can't we put them on here?'

Kitty answered this one. 'Because if people see you dressed as a bank van driver and a bank teller and, a few hours later, two men dressed as a bank van driver and a bank teller rob a bank, they may draw a link between the two.'

'Your outfits are in these bags with the burnt cork,' I said. 'Put them on over your regular clothes when you get to the Bog Road, so you don't leave any evidence.'

'But we'll be so hot!' moaned Ronan. As he said this, he spilled some tea on his leg. 'Ow!'

We were all feeling anxious now.

'I've picked the carrots and put them in a bag,' said Kitty.

'What are you two going to do with yourselves?' Derm asked.

'We might go for a cycle or sit on a beach,' said Kitty. 'We don't have a plan yet.' The truth was we were too nervous to think that far ahead.

'Just make sure you go in the opposite direction to us,' said Derm.

'We will,' I said.

'And if the police approach –'

We both spoke at the same time: 'WE DON'T KNOW ANYTHING.'

Soon it was time to say goodbye.

'T-Rex, thank you for your amazing plan,' Derm said as we hugged.

'Yes, thank you,' Ronan added. 'And remember: if it doesn't work out, it's your fault. And, if it does, don't worry about it.'

We all stared at him.

'No, wait,' he said. 'I meant the opposite of that.' He hugged Kitty and tripped on the door frame as he stepped outside.

'Good luck,' was all we could say now.

There were plenty of tears in our eyes as we watched them walk together down the driveway. But less when they came back up a few minutes later because they'd forgotten their disguises. Then none at all when they returned a second time to get the emergency sandwiches.

'Can you both help me with something in the shed?' Ronan asked, and Kitty and I dutifully marched in through the double doors.

Suddenly the doors swung shut behind us and were bolted from the outside.

'What's going on?' I shouted.

'I'm sorry,' Derm said, 'but this way, if we're caught, the police will know you weren't involved.'

'Sorry, Kitty! Sorry, Ray!' said Ronan. 'See you in a few hours. Hopefully – and, if not, we'll see you in a few years when we're all free again.'

'He's joking,' said Derm.

'I wasn't,' said Ronan, and we heard their footsteps crunch down the driveway.

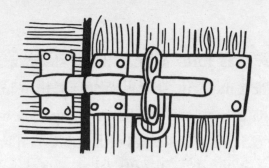

21

PRISONERS

An uncomfortable silence settled over the dusty mounds of junk in the shed.

To peer inside those doors was the closest you could get to peering inside my uncle's brain. A garden mower he had attached to the back of a bicycle sat beside a running machine he had built from a tumble dryer. A pile of unreturned library books sat on an old piano that had been converted into a two-storey dog kennel. Overlooking it all was a huge moose head mounted on the wall, with ropes and hoses of different lengths dangling from its antlers.

Kitty was furious. She would sit on a broken sofa for a moment, shake her head, then jump up and pace around, before flopping down again on an old pile of suitcases or an upturned bathtub. I sat on the floor in the corner. At one point she came over and grabbed my wrist to check the time, then muttered, 'This wasn't part of the plan!'

Derm and Ronan had left for the final time at 11.45 a.m. The walk would take about an hour, so they should be in position an hour early. That left plenty of time to round up the sheep and have them in place, even if the bank van was twenty minutes early. If it all went well, they should be back in two and a half hours.

'Let's play a game,' I said, and before she could say, 'Absolutely not!' I started. 'I spy, with my little eye, something beginning with C.'

'Absolutely not!' she said.

'Sorry, we've already started.'

Kitty was staring up at the little window high above the doors. 'I'm just worried that if it rains, their beards will wash off . . . Is it C for clouds?'

'There are no clouds,' I said. 'For once, it's definitely not going to rain today.'

'Clothes?' she said, pointing at her favourite rainbow T-shirt.

'Nope.'

'Case, as in suitcase?'

'No.'

'What if there are no sheep?'

'There will be sheep,' I said. 'This is Achill. There's always sheep.'

'Caribou then,' said Kitty, pointing at the moose's head.

'Good but no.'

Kitty climbed up on to a stack of three school chairs, then immediately jumped off and sat back down on the floor next to me.

'Clock?' she said, pointing at my watch.

I shook my head.

'What if the sheep don't stay on the road?' said Kitty.

'They will,' I said calmly.

'Of course they will,' said Kitty, sounding like she was arguing with herself. 'Sheep love Derm's carrots.'

'You got it!' I said.

'What?'

'Carrots!'

'Wait, WHERE?' She was looking around frantically.

'That bag of carrots on the table.'

Kitty leaped to her feet. 'That's the bag they were supposed to ... THEY'VE FORGOTTEN THE CARROTS! Oh no,' she wailed. *'Oh no!* If there aren't enough sheep, then the bank people will see them and *call the police!'* Now she was really freaking out.

She shoulder-charged the doors but they didn't budge.

'Help me with this,' I said, standing at one end of the kennel-piano.

'What are we doing?' Kitty asked.

'We're building a tower.' I nodded up towards the small window four metres above the doors.

We pushed the kennel-piano into position, then tipped out the contents of a wardrobe and heaved it on top of it.

I climbed up on that and scanned the room for the next building block.

'Three chairs,' I said.

'What?' Kitty looked at me, baffled.

'Three chairs!' I said.

'What, like hip hip –'

'No,' I said. 'Those school chairs!'

Kitty threw each one up individually and I stacked them in a triangle.

Carefully perching on the top chair, I could almost but not quite reach the window. I didn't dare think about the wobbling tower beneath me.

'Stay where you are!' shouted Kitty.

She climbed up on the kennel-piano, then on to the wardrobe, then up on the top chair so that she was directly behind me.

'On three, I need you to jump,' said Kitty.

'Maybe you should do it?' I said.

'I won't fit out of that window, but you might.' And, before I had time to think, she said, 'Three!'

As I jumped, Kitty grabbed my waist and lifted me high enough to be able to sit on the windowsill. I slid the window open and moved my legs round so that they were dangling outside.

It was a big drop down to the ground.

'Rex!' Kitty said. I was expecting her to tell me to hurry up, but she didn't. 'Don't jump if you think you'll hurt yourself.'

But a little to my right was Derm's van. Its roof was only half the distance to the ground. It was still far – the biggest jump I'd ever done, but it was doable.

'I can do this!' I said. 'I can definitely do this.'

'Amazing!' she said.

'Actually, I'm not sure I can.' Doubts were starting to fill my head.

'STOP THINKING ABOUT IT AND DO IT!' yelled Kitty. 'THREE, TWO –'

CLUNK. I landed on the roof of the van and checked my legs – yep, they were still a hundred per cent intact. I slid down and unbolted the shed.

Kitty was ready with the carrots in a bag on her back.

'You did it, Rex!' She grab-hugged me, and five seconds later we were on our bikes, racing down the hill.

22

WE'VE GOT THIS

We cycled faster than we'd ever cycled, taking it in turns to be the one in front, each time trying to go a little faster.

We reached the Bog Road at 1.55 p.m. I was worried that we might have missed the van or that Derm and Ronan would be difficult to find, but three sheep were munching their way through the emergency sandwiches in the middle of the road.

'Kitty!' Ronan's face, with the addition of a very badly drawn-on moustache, popped up from the ditch on one side. He looked like an old-fashioned inventor or a footballer from the 1980s.

'Rex!' Derm popped up just across the road. His even more ridiculous drawn-on beard made him look like he'd been living alone on a desert island for ten years. Even though we were the only non-sheep for miles, they still both spoke in loud whispers.

'You're not supposed to be here!' said Ronan. *'But did you bring the carrots?'*

'You have to get out of here!' said Derm. *'Just after you've helped us.'*

'Stay where you are!' Kitty called back. 'We've got this.'

We were still both panting from the bike ride, but this was one of those times when you don't notice how tired you are because you have such an important job to do. I hid the bikes behind a bush that was far enough away while Kitty tipped the big bag of carrots out into the middle of the road. Then we began breaking them up and spreading the bits across the width of the road.

Realizing something more delicious was on offer, the three sheep abandoned the sandwiches. They must have signalled to their friends because suddenly at least twenty more came from nowhere, bumping me and Kitty on our knees as we prepared the rest of their feast.

In the back of my mind was the fear that this could all be a mistake. What if Friday had been a one-off and the bank van didn't usually come this way? Then our whole operation would have been a huge waste of effort and carrots.

This thought was interrupted by Ronan, this time whisper-screaming, *'IT'S COMING!'*

Kitty and I looked up over the backs of the sheep. It reminded me of when you go above the clouds in an aeroplane. Well, it was like that, but with a blue bank van in the distance, zooming towards us.

It was happening. And Kitty and I were definitely not supposed to be here.

'What do we do?' I whispered in her ear.

'I don't know!' she said, shaking her head vigorously.

If we stood up now, we'd stick out against the backdrop of white woolly coats.

'We have to stay put,' she said.

'OK,' I agreed. It was our only option. As more sheep arrived and swarmed round us, we lay flat on the road beside each other and held hands.

Ronan and Derm might have been shouting at us, but we couldn't hear over the sound of carrots being crunched and our hearts beating in our ears. After what seemed like an hour but was probably a minute, we heard the first beep of the van, then a burst of three, followed by one long, sustained *BEEEEEEEEEEEEEP*.

Just as a level of utter panic I'd never known before rose inside me, Kitty leaned into my ear and said calmly, 'Don't worry. I'm sure nothing bad will happen. Nothing *baaaaaaaaad.*'

Then, taking Kitty's lead, all the sheep around us started baaing as loudly as they could. I joined in too. A week before, I'd been terrified of them. Now I was part of a flock.

23

THE HEIST

From that moment, everything went as well as we could have hoped.

We heard Driver open his door and jump out, leaving the engine running as he tried to hoosh the sheep away. But we didn't budge. Around us, there were still a lot of carrots to be eaten. Then Pointy got out to help.

This was the cue for Derm and Ronan, who jumped up from their hiding places. They leaped into the van and locked the doors. While the baffled bank staff froze, Kitty and I manoeuvred our new woolly friends a little nearer to the side of the road and, when there was enough of a gap, the van roared through.

Just as I was starting to think of the exceptional excuse we'd need to give Pointy and Driver when the sheep left and they found us lying on the road, I heard the bank van screech to a halt thirty metres away. I peeked up and saw Ronan's arm frantically waving out of the window.

'*Let's go,*' I whispered to Kitty and didn't wait for a response.

I can only imagine how surprised Driver and Pointy were when two humans suddenly popped up out of the sheep and, with their T-shirts pulled over their heads, sprinted in through the big back door of the van and it sped off again.

I was happy to be back in the tick-tocking calm of that perfect, tiny bank. It felt a million miles from the frenzy of the last few hours. Kitty and I took a few deep breaths and made our way round the counter.

'Keep your heads down!' Ronan barked. Poor Ronan. He wasn't dealing very well with all this stress. I could see his whole chest rising and falling each time he breathed in and out. He glanced over at us, then yelled, 'STOP SMILING – THIS IS VERY SERIOUS!'

We were smiling because Ronan and Derm's sweat was causing their moustache and beard to drip down their faces. It looked like they were melting. A momentary crackle from the van's walkie-talkie on the dashboard made Ronan yelp, then throw the radio on the floor and stamp on it for way too long.

'Calm heads, please, everyone,' said Derm, who continued to be remarkably relaxed. 'We're nearly home.'

'Yeah, chill out, Dad,' said Kitty.

But Ronan wasn't able to relax. 'What were you two doing on the road back there? That wasn't in the plan!' he shrieked.

Kitty fired straight back: 'Funny you should say that because I don't remember the part of the plan where you were supposed to lock us in the shed, or *forget the carrots.*'

'We had dealt with it! We'd used the sandwiches!' Now Ronan was waving his arms around wildly as he spoke.

'Three sheep weren't going to stop that van!' said Kitty. 'And sheep don't even like cheese sandwiches. They come from their friends: cows!'

'Guys!' I said. 'This is really, really bad.'

'What now?' Ronan growled.

I nodded at the road up ahead. A car was parked to one side – a car with a stripe around it and two blue lights on the roof. And standing in the middle of the road, with his back to us, was Sergeant Crummey.

24

CRUMMEY TIME

'Oh, this is really, really bad. Really, really bad!' howled Ronan. He was getting hysterical.

'Ronan,' Derm said sternly, 'I need you to shut up now, sit still and pretend to be calm. Thank you.' It may have been the only time I ever heard my uncle raise his voice, and even then he did it in a polite way.

It was what Ronan needed and he nodded.

Derm went on. 'Rex and Kitty, get in the back and stay there. Remember, this is Crummey we're dealing with. I will handle it.'

I wasn't sure how he planned to do that, but this was my uncle. And he was extraordinary.

We'd put sunglasses in their inside pockets, and they both had them on their faces as Derm brought the van to a halt, just behind the sergeant.

Kitty and I peeped over the counter to see what was going on.

Tourists and locals lined the crossroads up ahead as trucks and tractors pulled brightly coloured homemade floats past and lines of girls and boys in majorette costumes twirled/dropped/picked up their batons. Of course! It was the closing parade of the Summer Festival.

'Quick as you can!' Crummey was roaring at them. 'I want to get this road open soon so I can go home for my soup!'

A flat truck was passing with the Achill Island Archaeology Society's float. They had built a cardboard replica of Grace O'Malley's pirate castle and the group's members stood around it, dressed as medieval pirates. Just then a wayward baton from a tiny majorette bounced off Crummey's head.

For a moment, I thought he might arrest her, but, as he turned round to pick it up, he noticed our van. He had to raise a hand to block the glare of the afternoon sun to see who we were, but, once he read the sign on the front, he raised a finger and made his way round to the driver's side. Derm opened his window a quarter.

'Another half-hour and we'll be done,' said Crummey, still gazing off in the other direction. 'Twenty minutes if I can get them to hurry up a bit.'

We didn't have half an hour! By then Driver and Pointy would have found a phone.

'Yep,' said Derm calmly. Derm had no idea how Driver was supposed to sound, so he'd gone for an accent that was many things and none at the same time. In that one word, he had managed to sound Australian but also German.

'Do you have it?' asked Crummey.

'What now?' said Derm, this time in a more American-sounding accent.

'The item we discussed.'

'Remind me,' said Derm. He was trying to use as few words as possible.

Crummey lowered his voice. 'I want a Niall the Gnome moneybox. To keep the coins in, at the station.'

I couldn't believe it. Crummey wanted a free piggy bank! There was a display of them close to where I was hiding in the back, so I grabbed one and tossed it on to Derm's lap. He opened the window another half-turn and offered it out. Crummey seemed very happy and put it under his jacket.

'When did you change your route?' Crummey asked next. But, before Derm could answer, the sergeant was distracted. A familiar-looking figure in a black swimsuit with a yellow lightning bolt across it was stumbling out in front of the Achill Sub-Aqua Club float. She had, I would later find out, rubbed the red ink from the bank counter stamp all over her leg and sneaked out of the back door of the van.

'Help, Sergeant Crummey! I've been bitten by a shark!' Kitty shouted.

The supposed attack raised so many questions, not least of which was: if she'd just been bitten by a shark, how had she managed to run all the way from the beach to here?

But Crummey wasn't thinking of that. He saw his chance to be a hero.

'Stop the parade!' he yelled, and dashed over to help the victim. As he did, a gap opened up in front of our van. And, as all eyes were on Kitty, Derm put his foot on the accelerator and we were on our way again.

When we were far enough up the road, we all cheered.

I had to remind Derm to drive at normal speed a couple of times, but we didn't pass another person on the rest of the journey home. At the brightly coloured radiators, we checked to see if anyone was around, but it was just us and Duncan.

He let out a surprised *'EEEE-AWWWW!'* as he saw this new vehicle bump the gate open, and Derm floored it as we sped up the driveway.

And this is where I exhaled my deep, deep sigh of relief.

When we reached the house, I jumped out of the back door to open the shed. Derm wasn't paying attention and drove straight into the kennel-piano we'd used to escape earlier, sending the whole tower crashing to the ground. Ronan and I moved everything out of the way and soon we had shut the doors and the bank van was safely hidden inside the shed.

As I walked to the front door, I noticed that sheep had knocked over Derm's fence and were munching on his weird vegetables again. Today, I didn't think we could really complain.

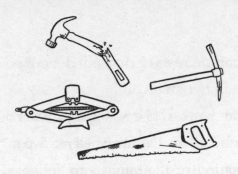

25

MONEY IN THE BANK

Ronan and Derm had washed off their facial hair and changed into their regular clothes by the time Kitty got back. She'd managed to convince Crummey that her running into the middle of the parade had been a protest to 'raise awareness of sharks'.

'A lot of people are swimming into them, and that's not fair on the sharks!' Kitty had told him. Crummey explained that he was only in charge of crimes that happened on land, and anyway he wasn't sure that swimming into sharks was a big issue as he'd never heard of it ever happening. In the end, he'd promised to raise it with his superiors and the parade restarted as Kitty walked back to the house in her swimsuit.

The four bank robbers – that's what we were now – gathered in Derm's shed at 5 p.m. for the grand opening of the van, to be followed by the even grander counting of the cash. Afterwards we'd eat our dinner and then bury the van when it got dark.

This time Ronan bolted the double doors shut from the inside.

'Not the first time today we've been locked in here,' said Kitty, looking sternly at the adults.

'Sorry about that,' said Derm as he used a long pole to pull the curtain across the window I'd escaped through. Now the only light was from the torch Derm was holding.

'OK,' Ronan said. 'Everybody put these on.' He held out four pairs of washing-up gloves. 'We don't want fingerprints anywhere.'

'Eh, Dad, we've all already touched everything,' said Kitty, 'loads of times. Anyway, I thought we were going to bury the van.'

'Fine,' Ronan huffed. 'You can touch it, but not too much.'

'Dad, are you worried that when we bury it, it'll grow into a bank-van tree, and each one of the little bank vans that grows from it will have our fingerprints on it?'

Ronan didn't answer. Instead he shoved the washing-up gloves back into his trouser pockets and looked away.

Derm led us round to the back of the van, then he paused for a moment. 'OK, everyone, I'd just like to say –' suddenly he clicked the torchlight on his own face – 'I'm a werewolf!'

Ronan recoiled in fear, but Kitty and I shook our heads. 'Basic error there,' said Kitty. 'Werewolves don't like light so a real werewolf would never do that.'

Derm rolled his eyes, then pushed the door open and we followed him inside.

Kitty and I glanced over at each other. We were both feeling the same mixture of elation and fear – it was like the night before your birthday mixed with the night before you get your school exam results. It could all turn out great and we'd saved the Old Coastguard Station. But there was also the chance that we'd spent the most nerve-racking day of our lives robbing an empty van.

'Can I just say –' Kitty stood in front of the counter – 'whether there's money in here or not, we did it and that deserves a moment of celebration.' She began to applaud, and we joined in. There were whistles and hugs, and Kitty got up on the counter and started ripping up bank leaflets and throwing them over our heads like confetti. I decided to join her, but, as I climbed up, my finger brushed against a button hidden on the underside of the counter.

The van jolted and for a moment the world seemed to stop. *CLU-CLUNK.*

You don't think you know what a large quantity of notes and coins falling through a metal door into a secure box sounds like, but then you hear it and say to yourself, *That's definitely the sound of a large quantity of notes and coins falling through a metal door into a secure box.*

'Oh no,' I said.

'Uh-oh,' said Kitty.

Derm slid open the drawer I'd seen Pointy take the money out of on the first day, but it was empty. Not empty as in no money, but empty as in the bottom had fallen out of it. Then he opened the cupboard underneath it, where I'd seen Pointy put the big bags of cash. The bottom was gone from that too. Underneath was a metal door that had slammed shut.

'Eh, where's the money?' Ronan asked in a strange, squeaky voice I'd never heard him use before.

'It's fallen into the drop safe,' said Derm.

'Oh no,' I said again.

'Uh-oh,' Kitty said again too. 'What's that?'

'It's an anti-robbery thing. When the panic button is pressed, the money falls through a spring-loaded trapdoor into a safe built into the bottom of the van. Did one of you press a button? They're usually under the counter.'

'I –' I was about to own up when Kitty interrupted.

'We both did,' she said. 'We both must have pressed it at the same time. Sorry.'

Ronan looked like he wanted to throw us into the ocean, but Derm, as usual, took it in his stride. 'Not to worry,' he said. 'We'll figure it out.'

Ronan wasn't coping. 'What do you mean, "not to worry"?' he screeched. 'We're about to have every police officer from here to Dundalk descend on this island to find this thing and you're telling us *not to worry*?'

'We've done the hard part, Ronan,' Derm said calmly. 'We've got the money. Now we just have to figure out how to get at it.'

'Do you think we can?' Kitty asked.

'We can do anything!' said my uncle with a beaming smile.

An hour later, Ronan and Derm had pulled out the wooden counter and removed most of the floor, leaving a large safe built into the steel chassis of the van. Derm's big torch had been replaced with the lamp from the kitchen table, which sat beside the bench where Kitty and I were sitting. She was leafing through banking brochures while I looked on anxiously. Some of Ronan's stress was starting to rub off on me.

'Maybe I could try to guess the code?' There were four dials on the side of the safe.

Derm looked up and smiled. 'There's about five million possibilities.'

'Well, if I start now . . .'

'Maybe you'll get it in about eight years,' said Kitty.

'We don't have eight years,' said Ronan, who was at the taking-everything-literally phase of distress. Every few minutes, he would thump the safe too hard with his hand and Derm would tell him to relax.

By 2 a.m. the floor of the bank van was littered with broken hammers, a cracked pickaxe, a bent car jack, two drills that had been used till blue smoke came out of them, and a blunt saw.

'Come on,' said Derm. 'It's been a long day and let's not forget that it went pretty well. We'll sleep on it and, who knows, maybe the solution will come in a dream.'

26

THE STORY
ESCALATES

'And did ye hear about yesterday?' Roisín asked as
Kitty and I stood at the counter of her shop
next morning. We'd come down to get breakfast
things for Derm. He'd be exhausted after yesterday's
exertions.

We shook our heads.

'You know that bank van that goes round the
island?'

We nodded.

'It was robbed . . . by an armed gang!'

'Like armed as in guns or they just had arms?'
Kitty asked.

Roisín shook her head and made pistols with her hands.

'Wow,' I said.

Roisín told us the whole tale. 'They stopped the van by machine-gunning the tyres – *dadadadadada.*' She really went for it with the sound effects and her whole body jolted as she fired her invisible machine gun. 'Then they forced the staff out and drove off in it.'

If only she knew that the only weapons we'd used were carrots.

'But hang on!' said Kitty. 'If they shot the tyres, how did the van drive away? Vans won't drive after they've had their tyres shot.'

'Good point,' said Roisín. 'They probably loaded it on to a special truck, or a helicopter . . . Yeah, that's it – a helicopter swooped down!' She was getting really carried away now as she swirled one hand over her head like rotor blades. 'They picked it up, maybe with a sucker thing or a big claw from a funfair, and flew away.'

This time I nodded because I didn't know what to say. The story had escalated so quickly.

As we walked back up with the food, Kitty opened the gate into Duncan's field. 'I feel that a swim at this point will clear our minds,' she said, and before I could object she was jogging in the direction of her castle.

She was already in her swimsuit by the time I got to the bottom.

'We'd better not stay down here too long,' I said.

'Rex, I always do my best thinking when I'm swimming. Maybe if we both get in, it'll double our brain power!'

'Really?'

Kitty nodded.

'But I don't have my –'

'UNDIES! UNDIES! UNDIES!' Kitty chanted.

I thought of Mum and her fears, then I looked over at Kitty. She was standing at the edge of the pool, doing made-up ballet poses, facing the cave opening and the sea.

I pulled off my T-shirt and threw it on the ground. Then unbuckled my belt and kicked off my shoes.

Kitty turned round and started to applaud. 'Are you ready to do this?'

'I think so,' I said, as I made my way to the water's edge.

'Eh, Rex, your socks,' she said.

'Oh yeah.' I pulled them off and threw them back over my shoulder.

'Three steps forward and you'll be a sea swimmer,' she said.

'But they're such hard steps!'

'Let's do it together,' Kitty said. 'You want to open that safe, don't you?'

I nodded and she grabbed my hand. I took a deep breath and we both stepped forward one. Water now covered my ankles.

'Is this swimming yet?' I asked, my voice quivering.

'No!' We took another step.

Now the water was around my knees and it felt very cold.

'It's nice when you're in, I promise,' said Kitty.

'What if I'm swept out to sea?'

'There is no current in here.'

'What if I freeze?'

Kitty shook her head. 'Do you want me to get the rubber ring?'

'Yes!' I said, then immediately changed my mind. 'No! Wait . . . I have to do this properly!' I was about to take another step when I felt something brush against my foot. 'Crab attack!' I yelled, and jumped back two steps on to the gravel.

'Nobody has ever been attacked by a crab,' Kitty said. 'Nobody in the history of the world. I bet it was seaweed.'

I looked down into the water and saw that Kitty had been right. It was a lump of seaweed that had floated by. But my confidence was gone.

'Next time I'll get in,' I said.

She marched forward and was soon doing an elegant breaststroke around the pool. 'Rex, you have to stop overthinking everything. You've just robbed a bank. You can do anything!'

I sat down on the stones, as Kitty went on. 'Like, if we could lift the van up and drop it, the safe might smash open.'

'But the van has petrol in it,' I said. 'The whole thing might burst into flames.'

'A controlled explosion then,' said Kitty. She had flipped over and was now doing the backstroke. It looked like fun.

As she swam through a beam of light, she flicked her wet hair to the side and the spray from it made a rainbow.

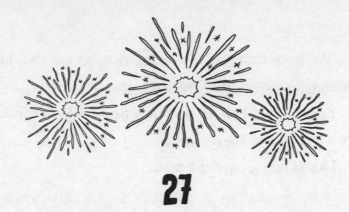

27

BOOM-BOOM

'We definitely shouldn't be doing this,' I said as Kitty taped another of Derm's fireworks to the front of the safe.

'One bang and that door is off!' she said.

I didn't like it. 'One bang and this shed is on fire.'

'Come on!' said Kitty.

'Let's run it past Derm,' I said.

'No, no, he's resting. We can't disturb him!'

'Well, he won't be resting if he hears his shed explode.'

Kitty stopped for a moment. 'Look, I want to make up for us getting the money stuck in there.'

'We both took the blame for that, so we should both get a say in this. We're a team.'

Kitty thought about it. 'But –' She couldn't think of a but. *'Fiiine.* We're a team.'

I liked being part of a team.

Derm was sitting up in bed, sketching something, when we brought his breakfast in. Ronan was over at Derm's desk, trying to fix the walkie-talkie radio from the van that he had stamped to death.

'Kitty was thinking –' I began.

Kitty cut across me. 'We were both thinking –'

I continued. 'That maybe the best thing to do would be to blow the safe open. Like with an explosion.'

'I mean we're never going to guess the right numbers,' added Kitty.

'And we can't smash it open.'

'Right,' said Derm, nodding. 'But what are the main dangers of blowing something up?'

'You could blow yourself up,' said Kitty.

'That's one,' said Derm.

'You could blow the van up and all the money too,' I said.

'That's another. Also, Sergeant Crummey and every other person on the island would know that something was going on. Everyone will have heard about the robbery by now, and they'll be on the lookout for suspicious activity.'

If Roisín was anything to go by, that would certainly be the case.

'If we were to blow it open,' Derm continued, 'we'd need to do it in the middle of nowhere.'

It was hard to think of a place more in the middle of nowhere than where we were, but Derm seemed to know one.

'You remember my friend Boom-Boom?'

'At the fundraising day!' said Kitty.

'He blows stuff up,' I said.

'Yes,' said Derm. 'And he doesn't ask too many questions, if you know what I mean.'

'What, like none?' said Kitty, glancing over at me with a smile. 'He never even asks how you are?'

Derm ignored this. 'He works in a quarry outside Manulla – that's about thirty minutes over the bridge on the mainland.'

'But will people there not hear Boom-Boom doing the – you know – *boom-boom*?' Kitty asked.

'Manulla makes this place look like downtown Tokyo,' explained Derm.

Kitty had another good question. 'But how will we get the van there? We can't just drive it across the island.'

'This is how.' Derm turned round the picture he'd been working on.

It was a white van with *Ice Cream* written on it. The giant plastic cone from above my bedroom door was mounted on the roof. Two people, one of whom looked a bit like Kitty and the other a bit like me, were serving ice creams through a hatch that had been cut in the side.

'It's going to take a bit of work,' said Derm, 'but if we start now, I think we'll be ready by tomorrow evening.'

'Genius!' said Kitty.

'Wait.' Ronan hadn't been paying attention, but had just looked up and seen the drawing. 'That ice-cream truck must be huge if we're going to get the bank van inside it.'

'No, Dad,' said Kitty, shaking her head. 'Just no.'

28

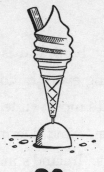

28

BANK VAN
ICE CREAM

Ronan burst into Derm's shed at 11 a.m. the next morning just as Kitty and I finished painting the van, and Derm was using his incredibly noisy circular saw to cut a window in the side.

'Big news,' he panted. 'So, I've just had a haircut . . .'

'Not sure I'd call that big news, Dad,' said Kitty. 'You didn't get much off.'

'I'm not finished,' said Ronan. 'So they've drafted in hundreds of extra police.'

'Hair police?' said Kitty, but he ignored her.

'They're sure the bank van is still on the island so they're searching every building. They said the thieves are Ireland's most wanted criminals!'

'Not a problem,' said Derm, pulling up his protection goggles. 'Ireland's most wanted will be out of here by five. Ronan, here are some stencils. Write something along the side to make it look like it sells ice cream.'

By noon Ronan had used the stencils to neatly write **ICE CREME,** which we then painted over and spelled correctly.

'We should give it a name,' said Kitty. 'Ice-cream vans never just say "Ice Cream" – they're always "*Something* Ice Cream".'

' "Kitty and Rex's Ice Cream" would be a bit of a giveaway,' I said.

'Oh!' Ronan had an idea. 'How about "Bank Van Ice Cream"?'

There followed a moment where we all looked down at the ground.

'How about "Cat and Dog Ice Cream"?' I said.

Ronan wasn't sure. 'But people might think it's ice cream for cats and dogs and not buy any.'

'Dad, we're not trying to sell ice cream,' said Kitty.

'Oh yeah. Let's go with that!'

Kitty stencilled the name on the front.

'We should have some ice cream onboard,' she said to me afterwards. 'Just in case anybody checks.'

'Good idea,' I said. 'I'll go down to Roisín's and get some.'

'No, I'll make some,' said Kitty. 'You go buy some cones.'

When I arrived back twenty minutes later with twenty not-completely-fresh cones, Kitty's ice cream was already in the freezer.

We rummaged around in Derm's shed and found a white suit for him, and white aprons and caps for us.

At 3 p.m. the shed doors opened and Derm drove out in the gleaming white ice-cream van. To finish it off, we glued the giant ice cream to the roof while Ronan wired up a loudspeaker beside it. Then we stood back for a moment to admire our kind-of names. And, when Derm pressed play and tinkly ice-cream-van music played through the speaker, it actually made you want some. In a way, it seemed a shame that we were about to blow it up.

29

ROAD CONES

Ronan was following in his car to drive us back from Manulla, along with the money. That was after Boom-Boom had boomed, and we'd pushed what was left of the van into a very deep lake.

As we drove along, a nice breeze came through the new window – I say window; it was a hole.

The island was much quieter today. The Summer Festival was over and everyone was going home. No fairs, no parades and, from the middle of the Bog Road, Achill looked exactly as it always did. We were the only vehicle, and the only faces, apart from ours, were gnawing on grass that was turning yellow in the unusually dry weather. At this rate, we'd be an hour early for our appointment with Boom-Boom. But, coming up to the bridge, we joined the back of a long line of cars.

'Maybe vandals have opened it again?' I suggested, catching Derm's smirk in the rear-view mirror.

We were all looking through the windscreen, trying to figure out what was going on, and didn't notice a little girl with pigtails and chocolate on her face approach the side window.

'Hello, man and lady,' she said, startling me and Kitty. I'd completely forgotten that we were sitting in an ice-cream van.

'How can I help?' said Kitty.

'How much is a cone?'

'I'm afraid we've sold out,' I said.

'They're twenty cents,' said Kitty.

'What?' I said. 'No, they're all gone.'

'I've just found some more,' said Kitty. 'How many would you like?'

'I'll have two, please,' said the girl, ignoring me and handing over two twenty-cent coins.

'Grab a couple of cones there, erm, Dog,' Kitty said to me, and I reluctantly did what I was told. Then she scooped two balls of her ice cream from the tub and handed them over to the girl, who said thanks and walked off.

'*We could make some money here!*' Kitty whispered excitedly as Ronan got out of his car to see what was going on up ahead.

'Kitty,' I said. 'We're not a real ice-cream van!'

She ignored me because now a father and son were at the window, and behind them a queue of three others. People were getting out of their cars and everyone wanted an ice cream.

But, by the time the sixth ice cream had been sold, our first customer had come back. The girl was crying and had brought her mother.

'These taste horrible,' she said. 'We want our money back!'

'Uh-oh,' said Kitty.

'Have a refund!' I handed her a fifty-cent coin. 'And have another ten cents to make up for it.'

'What did you use to make this ice cream?' I asked Kitty when they'd gone.

'There was no sugar, so I used flour. And there wasn't enough milk, so I used, well, flour.'

'So we've sold these people frozen flour?' I said.

'No, there's water in there too!'

Ronan appeared at Derm's window. Even by his standards, he was extremely flustered. 'A special police unit is checking everything that goes over the bridge. They're looking for anything suspicious.'

I looked down at the safe sticking out of the floor by my feet. 'Maybe we should get out of here,' I said.

'Agreed!' said Derm. As he began to turn the van round, the giant plastic ice-cream cone decided to detach itself from our roof and bounce, loudly, across the road.

'Leave it,' said Derm, and we got away just in time. Our four other customers were marching back towards us and they did NOT look happy.

'Sorry! We were trying a new recipe!' Kitty yelled out of the window as we sped off in the opposite direction, towards Derm's shed, and the official closing down of Cat and Dog Ice Cream.

30

EVERYBODY LOVES ROWING

While Kitty's way of clearing her mind was to swim, Derm's was to sleep for ten hours. Both seemed to work, because the next morning my uncle had a brand-new plan, the first part of which involved the four of us going out in his boat for a quiz.

'How many islands are there in Clew Bay?' he asked from his place at the front.

'Oh, I know this!' said Kitty. 'Three hundred and sixty-five. One for each day of the year.'

'Correct!' said Derm.

Kitty and I were huddled together at the back of the boat. Between us, Ronan was swooshing a pair of long, thin wooden oars back and forth through the water.

'And what kind of boat is this?' was Derm's follow-up question.

'A currach!' I said.

'Correct! They've been the same design for so long because they're stable in rough seas and they can carry a lot of weight. That's useful when you're moving stuff from island to island. Sometimes you see ten sheep on one currach.'

'Is that when they're going on their holidays?' asked Kitty.

'They're going to *Braaaazil*,' I said.

'*Baaaali*,' said Kitty.

'*Cubaaaa*,' said Derm.

We all looked at Ronan. He was concentrating on rowing. 'Dad,' Kitty asked. 'Where do sheep go on holiday?'

'Oh, eh,' he panted. 'They don't go on holiday. They just stay in their fields.'

We all looked away and he continued rowing.

'Sorry to ask this, Derm,' Kitty began, 'but how is this helping us open the safe?'

'Good question!' said Derm. 'See that island over there?'

About four hundred metres in front of us was another pier, with a few white houses dotted around it – an island off an island off an island.

'Inishbiggle!' said Kitty.

'Correct,' said Derm. 'It looks close, but this channel is shallow and has a cross-current.' I noticed that Ronan was now breathing heavily and starting to get sweaty. 'It takes about twenty minutes to row there,' Derm went on. 'But it'll take even longer when we attach four currachs together and put the van in the middle!'

'Whoa!' said Kitty, and she was absolutely right.

'There aren't many people on Inishbiggle and no police,' Derm went on. 'Boom-Boom is going to meet us on the beach at the quiet end of the island at three a.m. tomorrow night. Afterwards we'll push what's left of the van into the sea.'

'Nice plan!' I said.

Kitty had one issue. 'But why are we rowing? I mean, couldn't we just use an engine on the boat?'

'Good suggestion,' said Derm. 'But engines are loud and we have to be quiet when we get close to those houses in the middle of the night. Anyway, everybody loves rowing.'

Ronan didn't look like he loved rowing. 'Can I stop this now?' he pleaded. His face had gone past fire engine into a shade similar to Angley.

'Kitty and Rex can take over, Ronan,' said Derm. 'We'll give them a rowing lesson.'

Wow. We were really doing this.

'We'll get an early night,' said Derm as we rattled back towards the house an hour later. 'Then we'll rest up tomorrow and, at midnight, we ...' He stopped.

'Oh no,' said Ronan.

'Oh no,' said Kitty.

'Oh no,' I said.

Parked at the bottom of the driveway was Crummey's empty police car. He had gone up to the house.

31

AN INSPECTOR CALLS

'Let me take care of this,' said Derm as the van came to a halt, just close enough to the front of the shed that no one could open the doors. It was still bolted shut, so Crummey hadn't been in there yet. He was trying to peer in through the kitchen window.

Derm climbed out. 'Inspector Crummey, what a treat!' This was classic Derm. He had moved Sergeant Crummey up a rank to make him feel more important. 'It's nice to know that local law enforcement is keeping us safe in these dangerous times!'

What had Crummey seen? We had no idea.

The tension of the situation was temporarily broken when Ronan went to follow Derm out of the driver's door, got his foot tangled in the seat belt and landed in a pile of leg-and-arm spaghetti at the sergeant's feet. Derm and Crummey helped him up.

'Kitty, Rex,' Derm said as we followed Ronan out, 'let me introduce you to the most important person on the whole island.'

We went to shake hands, but Crummey had started laughing to himself.

My heart skipped a beat. Had Pointy remembered me from when I tried to get money out and then recognized me when I popped up in the middle of the sheep?

'Why are you laughing?' Kitty asked.

'I was just thinking that I hope you two don't chase each other around a lot!'

For a moment, we all looked at him, baffled.

'You know, because Rex is a dog's name and Kitty is a cat's name.' There was a pause and then we all laughed, because that's what you have to do when you've just robbed a bank and you're not sure if a policeman is about to arrest you.

'I met the girl the other day,' he said, nodding in Kitty's direction. 'She was in the parade. And a very good costume she had too. A lot of people thought she'd been bitten by a shark. Not me, though. I knew she was raising awareness.'

'Any news, Inspector?' Derm asked, carefully changing the subject.

'I suppose you've heard about the robbery,' Crummey began.

We all shook our heads.

'The mobile-banking van was stolen.'

Kitty did a baffled face. 'A bank in a van?'

Crummey nodded. 'A gang of four men stole it. We don't have any descriptions beyond that.'

I was happy to hear this, but Kitty wasn't.

'How do you know they were men?' she asked.

'What?' Crummey didn't understand.

'They could have been women,' she went on. 'Certainly one of them could have been a woman.'

Crummey had a smirk on his face. 'Women don't rob banks.'

'Oh, they do! They can do everything men can do – usually better.'

For a moment, I thought Kitty was going to admit to the robbery, just to prove her point, but Derm moved things along. 'Where did they put the van?'

'That's what we're trying to work out,' said Crummey. 'I'm going house to house, reminding everyone to look out for anything suspicious. Have you seen anything suspicious?'

We pretended to think about it, then shook our heads.

'It must be exciting, though,' said Derm, 'to be in charge of the biggest case of your career.'

Crummey's shoulders sagged. 'They've drafted in a special unit from Westport for the investigation. Apparently, it's what they do when a robbery is above a certain amount.'

'How much did they steal?' asked Kitty.

Crummey leaned in, like he knew he wasn't supposed to tell us. 'They reckon there was over one hundred and fifty thousand in the van. It was the busiest weekend of the year for the pubs and Angley's hotels. That gang really knew what they were doing.'

We all nodded.

'So, if you're not working on that any more, what are you up to?' Derm asked.

'Yesterday another crime was committed, which, while not as bad as the bank robbery, is still very serious.'

'Oh really?' said Derm, raising an eyebrow in anticipation.

'An unlicensed ice-cream-vending vehicle was seen operating in the vicinity of the bridge. And they were serving what can only be described as substandard ice cream.'

'No!' said Derm. 'That's an absolute outrage! Anyone who jeopardizes the excellent reputation of Achill Island ice cream needs to be tracked down.

I'm delighted that an experienced inspector such as yourself is on the case.'

Again Crummey seemed pleased. 'This gang selling the ice cream had a very specific name that I learned through my investigative work.' He took out his notepad. 'Kate and Doug Ice Cream. It was written across the front.'

For a moment, I thought Kitty might correct him again, but she stayed quiet.

'Have you come across a Kate or a Doug? They may be Spanish. They left behind a giant plastic ice-cream cone that had Spanish writing on it.'

We pretended to think about it, then shook our heads. 'We don't know them,' said Kitty.

Crummey shrugged and turned to go back down the driveway, then stopped.

'Oh, while I'm here, as part of this robbery investigation, every building on the island big enough to hold a van has to be checked. Can you let me see inside your shed for a moment, just so I can tick it off the list?'

We all froze.

'What?' said Derm.

'Just so you don't get bothered by anyone else.'

Nobody was saying anything, so I blurted, 'Let me try to find the key,' and began to walk towards the front door.

'We haven't been able to find it for a while,' said Kitty, following me. 'I'll help you look.'

'I'll assist Raymond and Kate . . . I mean, Kitty,' said Ronan.

We all had the same idea – our only way out of this was to leave Derm alone with Crummey, so he could work his magic.

When the three of us had walked calmly in through the front door, Ronan and I huddled underneath the window where we could follow their conversation.

'It's really bothering me,' Derm began, 'that you aren't leading the investigation into the bank robbery.'

'I know,' said Crummey. He sounded so disappointed.

'It's an OUTRAGE,' Derm went on. 'Nobody knows this island like you. Nobody understands island life like you do! I'm going to write a letter to the Chief of Police in Dublin right now!'

'What will you say?' asked Crummey.

'Dear Chief of Police, in these troubled times, when the security of our nation seems constantly under threat from these amazing super-criminals, we need our best and brightest defending us. Our best and brightest such as Inspector Crummey of Achill Island –'

Crummey interrupted Derm here. 'Can you say Sergeant Crummey? That's the name they know me by.'

'They say that the cream rises to the top,' Derm continued, now tracing out the words of his imaginary letter in the air with an imaginary pen. 'Well, on Achill Island, we see that cream every day, keeping us safe from harm, never going sour and lumpy. So please, for our safety and the safety of the people of Ireland, put him in charge of the bank robbery investigation!'

'Wow,' gasped Crummey. He was taken aback by the power of Derm's letter.

'You have to write to them too!' Derm added.

'OK, I will!' said Crummey, clenching his fists.

'GO AND DO IT RIGHT NOW, while your anger is still strong!' yelled Derm, gently pushing him back down the hill towards his car.

'I WILL!' said Crummey. He took a few steps forward before turning abruptly. 'I'll just check inside the shed first.'

Derm's plan hadn't worked, but before he could say another word the radio on Crummey's belt crackled into life.

'Sergeant Crummey. Come in, Sergeant Crummey.' It was a woman's voice.

He grabbed it off his belt and held it up to his mouth. 'Hello, yes, Sergeant Crummey here, over.'

'Return to base immediately. I repeat, return to base. There has been a major breakthrough in the ice-cream investigation. Over.'

'On my way,' said Crummey enthusiastically.

As he marched back down the stony driveway, Ronan and I emerged from the house with the sad news that we hadn't been able to find the key. Kitty came out a few moments later.

'That was very lucky,' said Derm.

'Yeah,' said Kitty. 'Lucky that Dad fixed the walkie-talkie in your bedroom.'

We all turned slowly to look at her. She had saved the day.

'He'll be back soon, though,' said Derm after we had congratulated her. 'And next time we won't be able to put him off going into the shed. We're moving tomorrow night's boating expedition to tonight.'

32

THE BANANA PIRATES

The pier sat at the end of a winding road that took you past homes, shops and a school that was not much bigger than Derm's house. And, when I say the picr sat at the end, I mean, if you weren't paying attention, you could easily drive down the ramp of the boat slip and into the channel that separates Achill Island from Inishbiggle.

Kitty and I had spent the evening painting the bank van yellow and drawing a big picture of a banana on the side. This had been Kitty's idea. Derm had said to cover over the ice-cream paint job with 'something inconspicuous' and I'm not sure Kitty knew what 'inconspicuous' meant.

It was an exceptionally still and bright night. A huge crescent moon floated over the pirate castle and lit the darkness so much that I could see that the grass that usually leaned to the side in the wind was standing straight up. I looked at my watch. It was 12.21 a.m.

'*Guys, can you keep it down over there,*' Derm whispered.

Kitty and Ronan were having a heated argument about the best way to tie Derm's boat to the other three he had 'borrowed' from the pier. I wasn't sure what excuse we'd have if somebody came down to see what was going on. The idea of a late-night banana emergency on Inishbiggle seemed a little far-fetched.

Soon the boats were roped together – two at the front and two at the back – and were bobbing in the water at the bottom of the boat slip. It was time to load the van.

Derm had brought two long planks of wood and positioned them from the wheels of the van to the front of the front two boats.

He put Ronan in the van driver's seat, in charge of steering and braking, and he sent Kitty and me round to the back of the van to push. 'We're going to do this very, very slowly,' he said, 'so listen for my instructions.' Then he climbed up on to the roof of the van, where he could see everything.

'Aye aye, Captain *Daaaarm*,' Kitty said. Then she turned to me. 'You realize we're pretty much pirates now.'

I hadn't thought about it, but yes – treasure, boats, gunpowder – this must be like what happened at the castle 500 years before. With the addition of a banana van.

'Ahoy, Kitty Catbeard,' I said, and she laughed.

'Yo-ho-ho, Shark Bait Rex,' she said back, and I laughed too.

'Let's try not to make too much noise,' said Derm and then, perfectly on cue, Ronan went to give a thumbs up, but his elbow hit play on the tape machine that was still wired to the big speaker on the roof of the van.

For a moment, tinkly ice-cream-van music echoed out across the channel. The volume of the music was matched by Ronan shouting, 'WHERE IS THAT COMING FROM?' until Derm yanked the wires out of the back of the loudspeaker. This was the one-thousandth reminder that, despite what Crummey and everyone else thought, we were definitely NOT a gang of criminal masterminds.

When we were all in position, my uncle gave a *three-two-one* and Kitty and I pushed the van the first few centimetres along the planks, till Derm knocked on the roof, which was the signal for Ronan to hit the brake. Then Derm checked everything was still aligned and we did it again. Very slowly, the van was making its way on to the boats.

Ten sheep sounded like a lot; forty sheep sounded like even more. But this was a big van with a heavy safe. And 150,000 euros onboard.

The small boats started to make large-ship creaking sounds as the van moved closer to the front. After ten minutes, we were nearly there.

'OK,' whispered Derm, *'this is the last bit, so let's just hope –'* He didn't get to finish the sentence because, at that moment, the van jolted forward and the two planks left the ground in front of us. Had we pushed too hard? Had Ronan forgotten to brake? Had Derm been knocked off? We ran round to the side, expecting the worst.

The yellow van was sitting perfectly balanced on the four currachs, with my uncle standing proudly on the roof, his arms raised in victory.

33

THE INISHBIGGLE
WIGGLE

While our van was definitely floating, it was clear that the boats were overloaded. The water lapped dangerously close to the top of their sides. Still, Kitty and I climbed aboard in our enormous life jackets and sat holding our oars in the back corners.

'OK, *everyone, gently does it,*' whispered Derm. '*GO!*'

We started to row – not the full strokes we had learned earlier, but more tentative ones, not wanting to put stress on the ropes that – from the creaking sounds we could hear – were not very happy to be doing the job they'd been given. But progress was being made, and the light breeze was pushing the van along like a sail.

Then the cross-current hit. Now I could understand why Ronan had gone so red. The current was forcing us left, towards Kitty and Ronan's side, so, in order to reach Inishbiggle, which was straight in front, we had to aim far to the right.

As always, my uncle remained upbeat. 'Stick to the same rhythm and we'll get there!' he called out. 'One-two, one-two.' Then he turned it into one of his awful songs.

> 'We won't row in a straight line,
> We'll row in a kind of a
> Squiggle squiggle,
>
> As we go
> On our way to Inish-
> Biggle Biggle.'

This was the worst one ever. And it wasn't finished.

'Move your arms,
Make your bum
Wiggle wiggle,

As we go
On our way to Inish–'

'You're actually making it harder,' Kitty said.

'Yeah,' I agreed.

'I quite liked it,' said Ronan.

'FINE,' said Derm in his mock-hurt voice. 'Democracy wins.'

Ten minutes later, we were still making headway, but it was slow. The sea had got considerably bumpier and the wind had switched direction. Now it was blowing into our faces.

'We're halfway!' said Derm. We gritted our teeth and continued.

Just then, a gust of wind brought a wave over my corner, drenching my arm and the watch Derm had given me for my birthday in February. This was at 1.03 a.m. I know this because my watch isn't waterproof and that's when it stopped.

Then another got Kitty. Just to be very clear, this wasn't the dramatic sailors-holding-on-to-ropes-for-dear-life storm you might be imagining. These were still small waves, but they were just big enough to get into our boats.

'Are we all still OK?' Derm shouted.

We said yes, but it was starting to look bad. The weight of the extra water in the boats was slowing progress even more.

I knew it was the beginning of the end when, in the water behind us, I noticed one of the ropes – its knot had burst open. From then, it didn't take very long.

'DERM!' I yelled, and he looked back to see another wave flood over my legs. Suddenly I wasn't really sitting in a boat – I was sitting in the water. And by sitting I mean floating in a life jacket. I was about to panic when I felt a hand in mine. It was Kitty. She had swum round to make sure I was OK. And then I felt Derm's arm around my waist.

It was the best angle to watch what happened next. As the boats dipped even more, the van began to roll backwards along the planks, slowly at first, then picking up momentum.

'Oh no,' said Ronan. 'I think I forgot to put the handbrake on.'

BLOOOB.

The van made the sound a big stone makes when you drop it into a deep rock pool. Or when you flop, bum first, into a bath. Or when a bank van full of money rolls into the sea.

It only took a moment and it was gone.

'I'm so sorry!' said Ronan.

'It's nobody's fault,' said Derm. 'We all did our best.'

But I could hear real disappointment in my uncle's voice. I knew what this meant to him, and for the Old Coastguard Station.

'Well,' Kitty said, 'at least we got Rex in the water!' And they all gave me a brief round of applause.

Without the weight of the van, our boats had come back up again. Ronan gave us each a bucket and we bailed the water out, then tied everything back together and rowed silently back in to the pier.

As our only means of transport was, well, not driving anybody anywhere, we had a long walk ahead of us in our wet clothes, in the dark. Derm was exhausted, so we sent Ronan on ahead to get his car and come back to collect us. Kitty and I did our best to keep Derm's spirits up as we ambled along.

As tomorrow was my last full day on the island, we talked about our highlights of the trip – Kitty's struggle to get all of the sheep into my bedroom on the first day, and then the expression on my face when I saw them; the fun we'd had organizing the fundraising day; Derm's strange accent when he was pretending to be Driver.

'It's just a pity it didn't work out in the end,' Kitty said.

'I think it still worked out pretty well,' said Derm, smiling at us both.

The sunsets on Achill are incredible, but I'd never seen a sunrise. At around 6 – I'm not sure exactly what time because my watch still said it was 1.03 – the sun burst like a volcano from the horizon and colour came into the world. First greys and purples, then greens and blues, and finally yellows and whites. I immediately felt my red sweatshirt start to dry out.

Ronan collected us in his car and dropped us back up at the house. I helped Derm to bed and made sure he took his last pills of the day. I'd never seen my uncle this tired before.

'Remember when I was babysitting and we made the waterslide?' he said as he rested his head back on the pillow.

I nodded.

'Well, look – now you're minding me.'

'Want me to build you a waterslide?' I asked.

'Maybe tomorrow,' he said with a glint in his eye.

I hugged my uncle and turned off his light.

34

IT'S NICE ONCE YOU'RE IN

'T-T-Rex,' Derm gasped as he heard my footsteps in the kitchen, next morning. Actually, it wasn't the morning, it was 2 p.m. And, by this point, I was very familiar with this tone of voice.

'*Rextinguisher! I . . . need . . . your . . . help.*' He said each word with a slightly more faltering tone and went back to his normal voice when he heard me click the kettle on. 'Good man! Can I have it in the orange teapot? And two scrambled eggs on toast.'

'What will happen now?' I asked as I delivered his breakfast.

'Well, I'll eat this and then probably have another sleep,' said Derm.

'No, with the Old Coastguard Station and the people who live there?'

'You mean the new Angley Old Coastguard Station Hotel?' said Derm with a rueful smile.

I nodded.

'Well, life goes on, T-Rex. Some people will go back to live with their families, I suppose. The problem is that some families won't be able to look after them. Some will have to go to other places, further away.'

'Where will you go?'

'I'm going to stay here.'

'No, but when the time comes. You could come and live with us!'

Derm shook his head. 'That's a very generous offer, but you and your mum need to get on with your own lives. There's a place in Dublin I could go to. The view isn't as good as here.'

'You should be able to stay in the place you love!' I said.

Derm smiled and shrugged his shoulders, before changing the subject. 'When was the last time you spoke to your mum?'

'Last week,' I said.

'Ring her today, won't you? You'll be home tomorrow and she'll blame me for keeping her Rexypoos from her.'

'I can't believe I'm going.'

'Well, make sure today is the best day of the whole trip,' said Derm. 'Do everything you've been wanting to do. Squeeze all the life out of it.'

I nodded. 'Can I borrow some money? I need to get something in Roisín's.'

Derm smiled the widest smile, reached under his bed and handed me a ten-euro note.

I marched down the hill in the sunshine to the shop. It was another beautiful day. Next thing, I was knocking on Kitty's window. She opened her curtains and smiled.

'Today's the day,' I said.

'Oh really!' She knew what I meant. 'Are we doing it?'

'We're doing it!'

The moment I reached the gravel at the bottom of the cliff, I kicked off my shoes. As I walked towards the water, I pulled off my T-shirt and then my trousers . . . to reveal my first-ever pair of swimming shorts.

'You got a pair!' said Kitty.

'Roisín's finest!' I said.

'This is AMAZING!' Kitty shouted. She was getting changed too, but not as fast as me. I had reached the edge of the water before her.

'Don't slow down!' she said. 'Don't think about it!'

For once, I didn't. I didn't allow myself to worry about the current or the cold or the crabs or the sharks. I stepped into the splashy puddle bit at the start – it was cold but I kept on going. Then I was lifting my knees to carry on at the same pace. There was a moment of fear as a few drops splashed in my face, but I didn't turn round – I did what I'd seen Kitty do. I dived underneath the surface.

Suddenly I was in a different world – a world that was silent and calm. I was moving in slow motion through the clear water. I thought about how I was in this huge puddle that went all the way across to America, all the way up to the Arctic – of all the boats and whales that were in it with me, the pirate shipwrecks ... our bank van. Just then Kitty grabbed me from behind and wrenched me towards the surface.

'What are you doing?' I panted.

'I thought you might be drowning!'

'No!' I said. 'I'm swimming!'

'You! Swimming!' She shook her head. 'Turns out you're a natural!'

I couldn't believe so much fun had been waiting here this whole time.

Kitty had brought the big rubber ring in with her. We both lay in it and paddled ourselves out through the mouth of the cave and the tide washed us in to Duncan's beach. Then we surfed in and out on the waves till our arms and legs ached with the best kind of tiredness.

Kitty turned to look out to sea as we made our way back up to the house. 'I can't stop thinking about the van sitting out there somewhere. Probably fish swimming in the big window. I suppose it's their money now.'

'Maybe,' I said.

'What do you mean?' said Kitty.

'I've had an idea.'

'You always get the best ideas while you're swimming! Is it a way of getting the money?'

I nodded.

'But you're going home tomorrow.'

'I know. We have to do it tonight. Just you and me. One last try. Are you in?'

Kitty smiled. 'Yeah, I'm in.'

'I hope you've been staying away from the sea,' said Mum, after we'd been chatting for a while.

It was time to be honest. 'Actually, I've just come from swimming in it,' I said.

There was silence for a moment. 'WHAT? . . . But think of all the terrible things, Rexypoos,' she said.

244

'Yeah, I've thought about them. I've thought about them a lot and I still did it. And I loved it.'

More silence.

'Oh, and, Mum,' I added.

'Yes, Rexypoos,' she said.

'Can you please stop calling me Rexypoos? Just call me Rex. I'm twelve.'

There was another pause. 'Ehm, OK. OK, Rex.'

35

AN INSPECTOR CALLS BACK

Crummey was back up at the house. This time he wasn't leaving till he'd checked the shed, so Derm was having some fun. He was standing in front of the double doors with his arms spread wide.

'Seriously, Superintendent, you can't go in there. There's something I really don't want you to see!'

'Stand aside, Dermot!'

'But I'm going to be in so much trouble!'

'I had my suspicions it was you. Open this door NOW!'

Derm put his hands above his head. 'Please don't shoot!'

'I don't have a gun. Now move!'

Derm gave us a wave when he saw us coming up the driveway and stepped to the side. Crummey karate-kicked the door, which didn't budge and clearly hurt his foot.

'It opens outwards,' said Derm.

Crummey scowled and pulled it open. Inside, everything was back to normal: kennel-piano over to the side; chairs in a stack; piles of everything everywhere.

Crummey was furious. He thought he'd cracked the case. 'Where's the van? What didn't you want me to see?'

Derm was shaking his head, pointing over to the piano. 'On top of that.'

Crummey ran over. 'These are just books!'

'They're library books,' said Derm. 'They were supposed to be back two weeks ago.'

'*Gah!*' Crummey howled.

'I'm *so* sorry. I just haven't had the time,' said Derm. 'How about I make it up to you another way? Maybe you'll stay for dinner? It's Rex's last night. We're going to barbecue some fish.'

Crummey stomped off down the driveway.

'Lovely to have met you, Chief Superintendent,' I said as he passed us, shaking his head.

I enjoyed my farewell dinner very much. Kitty and Ronan came up and so did Roisín.

After two weeks, I had learned that the best way to eat Derm's food was with your eyes closed. Then it was pretty delicious. We took the leftovers down for Duncan and he gave me a farewell dance.

I was booked on the next day's 4 p.m. train from Westport, so we needed to leave around lunchtime. Ronan said he'd come over if he was awake, but we both knew that was unlikely, so I said goodbye to him down by the road as Duncan looked on.

'You have some beautiful ideas in that brain of yours, Ray,' he said. 'Safe trip back to Dundalk, and please come and visit us again soon.'

I said I definitely would.

'Well, it's been so nice to meet you,' said Kitty. 'Thanks for not peeing on my carpet or chewing any of my stuff.'

'Thanks for not scraping your claws on anything.' And, as she came in for a hug, I whispered in her ear, *My window, two a.m.*'

36

IN THE
DRIVING SEAT

The trick to driving is that you have to remember to do a bunch of different things at the same time. You steer with your hands, occasionally shifting gears with one, while your feet do the stopping and the starting and the clutching. It's a bit like playing the drums except, if you stop concentrating for one second when you're playing the drums, there isn't a chance that you might veer off the road, drive into a petrol station that explodes and makes the whole village go up in flames. I'm exaggerating there a bit, but you get what I mean.

Derm had taught me to drive years before. In fact, the only vehicle I'd ever driven was his van. But that was on the beach. Not on the bendy roads of Achill.

At 2 a.m. I heard a cat meow and looked out of my bedroom window to see Kitty. We quietly opened the back door of Derm's van and loaded up the big bag and the box we needed for this mission.

'What's the plan?' Kitty asked.

'I'll tell you when we get there,' I whispered. 'Oh, and this time we're bringing this.' I was dragging the outboard engine for Derm's boat.

'Yes!' said Kitty. 'No more rowing!'

'And this.' I turned round to show her Derm's big torch, sticking out of my back pocket. She smiled ruefully.

I sat in the driver's seat and released the handbrake, while Kitty pushed from behind. The van caught the hill and Kitty ran round to jump in the passenger door as we rolled down.

'Go, go, go – start the engine!' she said.

'Shhhh!' I said. 'Operation Doughnut is a top-secret mission so there'll be no engine or lights till we get to the road.'

We bumped the gate open, and we were there.

I moved the seat as far forward as it would go, politely asked the engine to start and, when I turned the key, the van coughed into life. 'Thank you very much!' I said.

Kitty offered me a mint from the green tin on the dashboard.

'I don't mind if I do,' I said, and took two.

Then lights, handbrake, and slowly I lowered my foot. We began to move. First gear, second gear – I knew the trick with gears. When the noise gets too loud, move to the next one; when it's too quiet, come back to the last one. Gears weren't my worry – steering was. The roads on Achill were so narrow; I was hoping we wouldn't meet any traffic. But just past Roisín's shop we did.

The lights of the van picked out six ghostly green

marbles floating in the air that soon revealed themselves to be the eyeballs of three sheep having a rest in the middle of the road. I knew what Derm would have done here – pulled out the emergency harmonica and serenaded them away with a tune. But it was too late for that kind of noise. And, with the number of laws we were already breaking, it wouldn't be good to draw any more attention to ourselves.

Just as Kitty was climbing out to move them, she had a thought. 'How funny would it be if, when I got out, somebody jumped in, pushed you out and stole this van!'

I agreed, but I wasn't sure if funny was the right word.

Soon we were driving along the Bog Road again, near the spot where the action had taken place four days before. I was starting to relax – to get more confident with my driving – when Kitty yelled, 'Stop!'

I did what I was told and Kitty dashed off,

returning moments later with the two bikes I'd hidden behind a bush on the day of the robbery. She put them in the back and we both squealed with delight.

37

BANANATIME

'And this goes . . . here,' Kitty said as we lifted the engine on to the back of Derm's currach, which was floating at the bottom of the boat slip. 'You drove the van, so I'll drive the boat. Or steer it . . . or whatever you say. I'm an experienced sailor.' Kitty as boat captain wasn't filling me with great confidence. Also, something didn't look quite right.

'Shouldn't the propeller be in the water, not in the boat?'

'Good point,' she said. 'Let's move it round the other way.'

It was windier than the night before, and the sea was lumpier. But that wasn't going to put us off. This was our last chance.

We dragged the big bag onboard and put the box beside it.

'Now can you please explain what's happening?' Kitty asked as we zipped ourselves back into Derm's enormous life jackets.

'OK,' I said. 'It's low tide and the water is shallow in this channel, which means the van will be close to the surface. First thing, we have to find it – so let's do that.'

'I like it!' said Kitty.

We both grabbed an oar and used it to push the boat off from the pier, and, when we were far enough away from the houses that nobody could be woken up, Kitty moved to the back and pulled the starter cord. The engine nommed into life.

NOM NOM NOM NOM NOM

'Let's go!' she said, and we moved off.

Ten minutes later, we had powered through the current and were close to where the van had plopped into the sea. I remembered the exact spot because it was perfectly in line with the Inishbiggle pier on one side and the pirate castle on the other.

'What do we do now?' asked Kitty.

'Now we go fishing!' I said. I picked up Derm's big torch, rolled up my sleeve and plunged my arm into the dark water. The channel was only a few metres deep, so the powerful beam lit all the way to the sand on the seabed.

'Cool!' said Kitty.

Groups of tiny fish darted around in perfect formation, confused by our bright light. A larger one glided by, on its regular nightly business. But there was no sign of the big yellow whale that we were searching for.

'I think the current will have moved it that way,' said Kitty, pointing in the direction we were facing. 'Let's see where it takes us!' She shut off the engine and we started to drift.

I checked with the torch again, but this time the beam wasn't lighting all the way to the bottom.

'Maybe it's deeper here?' Kitty suggested.

'Maybe,' I said, but I suspected it was something else – something really bad.

My worst fears were confirmed the next time I checked and the torch barely lit halfway to the seabed. 'Kitty, our batteries are dying.' Without that one tiny component, our whole mission was destined to fail.

'OK, switch it off till I say,' said Kitty, and we moved on the current in silence for a few moments.

'Right – NOW,' she said.

'Are you sure? We might only have one more go at this.'

'I *feel* it!'

I plunged my arm in, switched on the torch and Kitty yelped, 'Bananatime!'

We were directly over a large yellow blob that was parked on the seabed. And with that our torch faded to nothing.

38

OPERATION DOUGHNUT

Kitty skilfully used the oars to hold the boat in position, as I began to pull out the contents of the big bag.

'Now explain everything,' she said, craning her neck to see what I was doing.

'This is Derm's doughnut,' I said. 'Remember? From the fundraising day.'

'Bouncyland!' said Kitty.

'And remember how we got it to go round the inflatable car?'

A huge smile broke out across Kitty's face. 'We can use it to raise the van!'

'Maybe,' I said. 'I'm not totally sure it'll work, but it's worth a try.'

'What do we do then?' Kitty asked. 'We still won't be able to get at the money.'

I went on. 'Remember how we both got on the rubber ring in your castle and the tide pulled us in to the beach?'

Kitty nodded.

'We can use the boat to tow it.'

'Ooh! Where, though? We can't just bring it back to the pier.'

'A secret place where it can be blown open and nobody will know – where the pirate queen used to count her plunder.'

Kitty clapped her hands and shrieked, 'My castle!'

I nodded.

'It's your greatest-ever plan, Shark Bait Rex.' And I gave a little bow.

'Now LET'S GO!' she said, and we set to work.

We put the airless doughnut into the water around our boat.

'OK, I'm going to do it,' said Kitty, and she began to unzip the tracksuit top she was wearing.

'No!' I said. 'You're the captain. You have to stay with the ship and keep us in position. I'm going to do it.'

Even as the words were leaving my mouth, I couldn't believe I was saying them. But then it was too late and I definitely had. A few moments later, I had stripped off and it was time for a second outing for my new swimming shorts.

'Don't think about it!' said Kitty, and I didn't. I jumped, feet first, into the dark water.

'It's actually *sooo* nice,' I said sarcastically as my teeth chattered.

'Don't stay in for too long! Oh, and look out for sharks,' Kitty said with a giggle.

'Eh, the ones you get here only have small teeth.'

Kitty was impressed. 'You've changed.'

'Maybe I have,' I said, grinning back at her.

I grabbed one side of the doughnut, took a gulp of air and dragged it downwards. The roof of the van wasn't far beneath the surface. I felt my way down the windscreen, down underneath the front bumper and shoved the section of doughnut under the front wheels. Then I swam to the surface for a few more mouthfuls of air.

'You're doing great!' said Kitty, not that she could see what I was doing. She gave me a thumbs up and I gave her one back. Then I went down to finish the job. I grabbed the opposite side of the doughnut and pulled it down under the back wheels. My guesswork had been roughly accurate – the ring was the right size to fit round the van. Then I found the inflation hose and took it back up to the boat.

Kitty reached out her hands and pulled me in.

'I did it!' I said, expecting her to be happy, but she seemed worried. My whole body had started to shake, and had we brought a towel? NO, OF COURSE NOT! Kitty took off her tracksuit top, wrapped it tight round my shoulders and engulfed me in an enormous hug.

'You did it, Rex,' she said, patting me on the back. I could feel her warmth through the summer rainbow T-shirt, and after a minute I'd stopped shaking. I gave Kitty back her now-damp tracksuit top and put my clothes on.

We removed the air compressor from its box and attached the hose.

'Here goes,' said Kitty. She pressed start and it putt-putted into life.

The air compressor was like a smaller version of the boat engine, except it pushed air down the hose. But would the van, now full of water, be too heavy to be lifted up? We would soon find out.

39

STARING AT
THE STARS

The doughnut would take a few minutes to fill. As the wind started to gust and the waves picked up, we lay down in the bottom of the boat.

'This time tomorrow I'll be looking up at the stars stuck to the ceiling of my bedroom at home,' I said.

'Oh, I have those stars too! I'll look at them when I miss you,' said Kitty.

I felt a few raindrops hit my face.

'This is the start of it.' said Kitty.

'The start of what?'

'When the nice weather breaks, there's always a –'

She didn't get to finish her sentence. From just beside us came an enormous crash of water.

'AAAAGH!' shrieked Kitty. We jumped up to see the banana/ice-cream/bank van floating on the huge inflatable doughnut.

'You did it!' said Kitty.

'We haven't done it yet,' I said.

We tied a rope round the doughnut and to the back of Derm's currach.

'Now let's see if it moves!' said Kitty.

'Full steam ahead,' I replied, and she started the engine. This time we moved forward till the rope became taut and we stopped moving for a second before . . . yes! We were moving again, and so was the huge trailer we were pulling.

Kitty put the engine to full power and, helped along by the current, we really started to pick up pace. Luckily, there was no one around to see us pass under the bridge.

'How long do you reckon it'll take?' I asked.

'Captain Catbeard estimates about half an hour. Depends what it's like when we get out of this channel and into the open ocean. If you're tired, why not have a sleep in our luxurious cabin?' She gestured towards the puddle that was forming on the floor of the boat.

I smiled as the rain grew heavier.

For the third time on our late-night adventures, Kitty and I were drenched. But that wasn't my main concern. As we moved around the coast of the island, we were suddenly exposed to Atlantic waves. Each one lifted us slowly and dropped us fast. And, each time we passed over the top of a wave, the van would disappear and I'd think it was gone, till it came crashing over a moment later. I was starting to feel unwell.

I leaned over the side.

'Uh-oh,' said Kitty. 'Doggy's first seasick!'

Right on cue, I threw up into the water.

'Try to stare at something on the land,' Kitty said. 'Something that's not moving.'

I tilted my head up and tried to focus, but it was hard to see anything in the dark. Occasionally, I could make out a beach, or a house with a light on, but it would soon disappear as we moved round the next headland.

'Hang in there,' Kitty said. 'We're so close! Look!' She was pointing at the rectangular shape of the Old Coastguard Station. 'There it is! We're going to save that!'

The waves were getting even bigger. The currach was either climbing up one or plunging down the other side.

'Please don't fall off now, van!' I said. 'Please don't break now, rope!'

As Duncan's beach came into view on our left, we went over the top of another wave and a flash of light appeared up ahead.

'Did you see that?' I said to Kitty.

She nodded. 'Very weird.'

'What was it?'

'I don't know . . .'

It was too far out to be a house, or even a person on the rocks with a light. As the rain pelted down, we crested another wave and there it was again.

'I think it might be another boat,' said Kitty, 'and I think it might be coming towards us!'

Over the next wave, I saw it. It was bigger than our boat, painted orange and blue, with a cabin on the front.

'I know what that is,' I said.' It's the lifeboat!'

'STAY WHERE YOU ARE!' said a voice through a loudspeaker. 'WE ARE COMING TO RESCUE YOU!'

'But what if we don't want to be rescued?' Kitty said to me.

'What do we do?' I asked.

'They're going to ask questions,' she said.

'So many questions.' I glanced back at the doughnut.

'We have to.'

'I know,' I said. 'I know we do.'

We both looked back one final time, then at each other. Our hands met and lowered on to the hose that was still connected to the air compressor.

'Three,' I said.

'Two,' said Kitty.

'ONE!' Together we pulled the hose as hard as we could and it disconnected. Immediately, air began to rush out of the doughnut.

'We were so close,' I said.

'So, so close,' said Kitty.

Twenty seconds later, the van leaned to the side and tumbled back into the Atlantic Ocean.

BLOOOB.

40

FAREWELL

The lifeboat crew were truly baffled when they pulled up alongside us.

'We were just out for a little jaunt,' Kitty explained. 'It was quite nice earlier and –'

I interrupted by leaning over the side for another barf.

The lifeboat's spotlight moved to the still-partially-inflated doughnut in the water behind us. 'What is that?'

'That's a giant doughnut,' Kitty said.

'Why have you got a giant doughnut?' asked the confused voice.

I piped up here. 'Oh, one of us would get in it and try to hold on while the other drove the boat – or whatever you say.'

The lifeboat person was lost for words. 'But . . . do you know what time it is?'

I looked at my watch. 'Ehm, three minutes past one?'

'No,' said the voice. 'It's four a.m. Who does this boat belong to?'

'His uncle,' said Kitty.

'And he let you go out in the biggest storm of the summer?'

'Well, he's asleep and we were just about to park it – or whatever you say – just there.' I pointed towards Duncan's beach.

'They're idiots,' said another voice from inside the lifeboat's cabin, 'but we'd better make sure they get in safely.'

The lifeboat guided us in as close to Duncan's beach as it could go. When the front of our boat bumped into the sand, we jumped out and were able to drag it up the beach to a safe place.

'In future, always check the weather and don't go out when it's bad!' shouted one of the lifeboat crew.

'Or when it's good!' shouted another.

'Lesson learned,' Kitty said, and we heard the huge motor of the lifeboat roar off into the night. Then we climbed the cliff, crept past Duncan, asleep in his bush, and stood in the middle of the road.

'This is close to the spot where we had our first conversation,' I said.

'And now it's where we're . . .' Kitty didn't finish that sentence, but started another. 'I probably won't call over in the morning. I'm . . . Well, I was going to say that I'm busy, but what I mean is I'll cry.'

I nodded. 'We were so close!' I said.

'Your idea was so good,' she said.

'But now Derm isn't going to be able to stay here.'

Kitty put her hand on my shoulder. 'Your uncle is amazing and always finds a way to make the best of things. And you're amazing.'

Two weeks before I'd have gone red and run away. Now I didn't. I looked into Kitty's eyes and smiled. 'You're amazing too,' I said.

'Hey, are you going to tell anyone about this?' she asked.

'About what?' I said.

'You know, when people ask what you did over the summer?'

'I probably won't mention some parts,' I said.

'What'll you say?'

'Just that I became friends with a donkey called Duncan.'

'And a cat called Kitty,' she added.

'Best friends,' I said.

Kitty nodded. 'Kate and Doug will always be best friends.'

I went to hug her. 'Sorry if I smell of puke.'

'I don't care,' she said. 'Cats and dogs often smell of puke.'

We hugged for a long time and then walked off in different directions.

41

THE BIGGEST SHOCKSPLOSION

'REX!'

I sat up in bed. It sounded like Kitty's voice, but she wasn't calling round this morning. I looked at the clock beside my bed. I'd slept in till 1 p.m. again.

'REX! HURRY UP!' It *was* Kitty.

I jumped up and opened the curtains. 'It's amazing!' she said breathlessly. 'You won't believe this!'

I threw on my clothes and, a minute later, was running down the driveway after her. The storm had passed and it was another beautiful afternoon. There was a rainbow in the sky, like the one on Kitty's T-shirt.

Four cars and a truck with a satellite dish on the

roof and **NEWS** written along the side were parked at the entrance to Duncan's field.

As I caught up with Kitty, a news reporter was filming his segment by the gate while Duncan peered over his shoulder.

'And, in the aftermath of last night's storm, maybe only this donkey knows where all that money is coming from. Luke Milo, Lunchtime News. Now back to you in the studio.'

'*EEEE-AWWW,*' said Duncan. He was absolutely delighted to be the centre of attention.

WHAT? I mouthed to Kitty. I felt something in my stomach that I thought for a moment might be another vomit, but then I realized it was the biggest s h o c k s p l o s i o n of my life. Sorry, *s h o c k s p l o s i o n*.

As we marched down through the field, Kitty spoke quickly. 'On his morning walk, your uncle found a twenty-euro note on the sand, and then another, and then loads more coming in with each wave. So he got Dad down and they gathered it all in sacks. They're hidden in the piano-kennel.'

My eyes couldn't have widened any more.

'After a while, a fisherman noticed money floating on the water, and now everyone knows.'

'Wait!' I blurted. 'Our van must have sunk on the rocks and the safe –'

Kitty put a finger to her lips. 'It must have burst open in the storm!' she whispered.

'Do they have enough?' That was all I wanted to know.

Kitty nodded. 'They have enough.' She hadn't wanted to cry, but now there was water running down her cheeks.

Below us, the beach must have had thirty people on it. With each wave, the last few notes would wash in – a five here, a ten there. Somebody from the crowd would rush towards it and Sergeant Crummey, in a pair of huge blue wellington boots, would try to get there first with his special police tongs. 'This is now police property!'

Derm was making his way up from the beach while Angley struggled to get down on his crutches.

'What the hell is going on? Is this something to do with you?' he asked Derm.

Derm was beaming. 'Nothing to do with me, Mr Angley. But who knows? It could be a miracle for the Old Coastguard Station!'

Angley slipped as he went past, stubbing his broken foot, just as Derm threw his arms round us.

'Crummey will have a long day. If it's washed up and nobody knows where it's come from, you can keep it. And nobody knows where this is coming from.' As he said it, his chin jutted out a little.

'Maybe it was the sharks,' said Kitty.

'Or pirates. Maybe the new Grace O'Malley,' I said, looking over at Kitty.

'Well, it's time to send one of those pirates off on his next adventure,' said Derm. 'Come on, Kitty – let's borrow your dad's car and drive T-Rex to the station and maybe, on the way, you can explain where my van is and how my boat ended up down there.'

Together we made our way back up to the house for the last time that summer.

42

THE GENIE

That was all three and a half years ago. And now I'm looking down over Duncan's beach again. This time, I'm with an even bigger group. There's Mum, Roisín from the shop, Irene from the Post Office, Rosie the chemist, some of the volunteers and staff from the Old Coastguard Station, Boom-Boom and Sergeant Crummey. Oh, and Duncan. He's resting his head on my shoulder. I'm holding Derm's favourite orange teapot and inside it are his ashes.

My uncle lived for three more extraordinary years. Two up at his house and one at the Old Coastguard Station.

REFURBISHED THANKS TO THE GENEROUS DONATION OF AN ANONYMOUS DONOR said the sign just inside the front door. They'd got it done within thirty days and Angley had to find somewhere else to put his hotel. I came down to visit every school holiday, and we had a thousand more adventures.

Derm passed away in his sleep, after his favourite meal of fish and weird carrots. He was surrounded by piles of books and articles torn from magazines, and photographs of his favourite people. On the table beside his bed was one from my last-night party. It was me and Kitty, each holding a Niall the Gnome Kidz Klub moneybox. It's on my wall now.

He told me that he didn't want a funeral. He wanted people to make something, and to think of him while they were making it. Ronan had done a painting of the view from Derm's house, but he'd dropped it so it had a hole in one side. Roisín had made up a tune on her violin, Mum had done a collage of different photos of them growing up.

And Crummey had found a rock that was shaped a bit like Derm's van. It looked like another van too, but I didn't mention that.

And I decided to write these pages you've been reading. I didn't mean for it to be this long – sorry. But I kept thinking of more bits that needed to go in. I'm going to send a copy of it to Kitty in London with my next letter. She's got a new little brother. They've called him Dermot.

It turned out that I really liked my new school. I met a bunch of people on the first day, and they're still my friends. We're all on the swimming team. Mum doesn't mind me swimming any more. She says I've swum out of my shell.

Dad comes back to visit whenever he can. They get on much better now. Mum is much more relaxed. She just calls me Rex.

I nod at Roisín, and as she begins to play her slightly out-of-tune music, I remove the lid of the teapot. There's a strong breeze blowing out to sea, so, when I turn it upside down, all the ashes fly out like a genie, scattering on to the beach and into the world.

Everyone gives Derm a round of applause and I put the lid back on. As the others stand, looking out, I turn to go back up through the field and Duncan follows me.

As I walk, I find myself making up a song.

> 'Even though
> You've gone away,
> You haven't really
> In a way.
>
> It always feels
> You're here with me.
> When I check the time,
> It's still 1.03.'

DOCTER NOEL ZONE
~presents~

DANGER IS EVERYWHERE

with the help of my neighbours
DAVID O'DOHERTY (words)
and CHRIS JUDGE (pictures)

WARNING!
NEVER READ WHILE
CROSSING ROAD/FLYING
HELICOPTER/WRESTLING
WITH LIONS

BEWARE!
BOOK HAS
SHARP CORNERS

CAUTION!
DO NOT DROP BOOK
FROM OPEN WINDOW
(UNLESS
WEREWOLF/VAMPIRE
IS BELOW)

A HANDBOOK FOR AVOIDING DANGER

'I dislocated my jaw laughing'
Eoin Colfer

'Imagine the Mighty Boosh
crashed into the Wimpy Kid'
The Times

Read on for an extract!

INTRODUCTION

~~~~~~

HELLO, READER.

My name is Docter Noel Zone and I am a

DANGEROLOGIST.

In fact I am

THE WORLD'S ONLY DANGEROLOGIST.

I know this to be true because

I invented the word **DANGEROLOGIST**.

So you could say
I AM THE WORLD'S GREATEST DANGEROLOGIST.

Or even:

DOCTER NOEL ZONE:
THE GREATEST DANGEROLOGIST IN THE WORLD EVER

Note also that I am **DOCTER**, not **DOCTOR.** A doctor has to spend years just learning to be a doctor. I gave myself the first name **DOCTER** so I could concentrate all of my energy on being a **DANGEROLOGIST.**

It saved a lot of time and hardly anyone notices the spelling.

～ WHAT IS A ～ DANGEROLOGIST?

While you probably see the world as an exciting place where you can go on adventures and ride your bike, a **DANGEROLOGIST** sees it as an awful place where terrible things can happen, **ALL OF THE TIME.**

HOW DID YOU BECOME A DANGEROLOGIST?

An excellent question. I used to work as a

SWIMMING-POOL LIFEGUARD.

The pool had all the usual safety restrictions:

- No diving
- No running
- No ducking
- No bombing
- No sneaky wees
- No lovey-dovey kissing

But soon I began to see lots of other dangers that people weren't being warned about:

WALKING around the side of the swimming pool is dangerous.

GETTING INTO THE WATER is dangerous.

SWIMMING ITSELF IS VERY DANGEROUS.

SO I BANNED ALL OF THESE THINGS.

In fact, I banned moving of any kind.

But then there was a new problem. If people don't move while they are in water, they sink to the bottom,

WHICH IS EVEN MORE DANGEROUS.

And then I realized the real problem with swimming pools:

WATER!

DEEP END

The answer was simple:
I GOT RID OF ALL THE WATER.

Soon nobody came to my swimming pool any more and it had to close down. **AND I WAS DELIGHTED!**

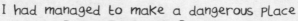

I had managed to make a dangerous place
NOT DANGEROUS AT ALL.

Thank you.

WHAT IS THE POINT OF THIS BOOK?

That is another very good question.

GOOD QUESTIONING!

1. To remind you that

DANGER
~ IS ~
EVERYWHERE

2. To make **YOU** into a qualified
DANGEROLOGIST (Level 1)

If you make it all the way to the end
of this book you will recieve a

DOD (Diploma Of Dangerology)
Level 1.

That means that you can make a
TINY CAPE OF DANGEROLOGY (T-COD)
and put the word **DOCTER** before your name.

And together we can show the world that

DANGER
~ IS ~
EVERYWHERE

Thank you.

Docter Noel Zone

THE GREATEST DANGEROLOGIST IN THE WORLD EVER

UNBELIEVABLY IMPORTANT!

★ SPLOD ★

(Special Protocol Language Of Dangerology)

As a **POD** (Pupil Of Dangerology) you will need to get used to the **SPLOD** (Special Protocol Language Of Dangerology).

The **LOAD** (Life Of A Dangerologist) can be very busy:

★ **LOFD**ing (Looking Out For Danger),

★ **POWDMB**ing (Pointing Out Where Danger Might Be)

and

★ **MSTDIDWEEIPSTIA**ing (Making Sure There Definitely Isn't Danger Where Everyone Else Is Pretty Sure There Isn't Any).

As you will see, this book contains a great deal of SPLOD.

Here is a quick guide to some of the basics:

DAD

In **DANGEROLOGY**, your **DAD** is not your father but your **D**anger **A**lerting **D**evice. This is a whistle, worn round your neck, that signals to other **DANGEROLOGISTS** that

there is **DANGER** nearby.

WARNING! Never toot your **DAD** at a football match. The players will all stop playing and everyone will be very unhappy with you.

BEWARE! Do not get a **DAD** with a toot that is too high-pitched. It could act as a signal to dogs in the area, making a dangerous situation even more dangerous.

PEBB

(Personal Emergency Bum Bag)

Every **DANGEROLOGIST** needs a **PEBB** around their waist, full of important **ADEGs** (Anti-Danger Equipment/Gadgets).

T-COD

(Tiny Cape Of Dangerology)

It's like a name-badge for

DANGEROLOGISTS.

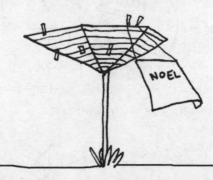

TID

(That's Incredibly Dangerous!) Something **DANGEROLOGISTS** say a lot.

NED

The opposite of **TID** is **NED** (Not Especially Dangerous).

The **SPLOD** we hold back
for rare occasions is:

RAD

which is **R**eally **A**wfully **D**angerous.

If your day looks like it might have anything **RAD**,
maybe you should **SIB** (**S**tay **I**n **B**ed).

RAD!